WEST OF THE PECOS

The Dukes were a mean, vicious family of killers, but they made one bad mistake. They left Matt Holder alive. Left for dead in the desert, and with his son killed, Matt is saved by the sisters from a desert mission. Once recovered, Matt sets out on a revenge trail into the bleak, harsh deserts and mountains west of the Pecos, but he soon encounters trouble.

He is arrested for murder but rescued by a group of Apaches he has befriended. Then, in Spirit Valley, comes the final confrontation between Matt and the Dukes, the outcome of which can only end in death and the odds are on their side.

West of the Pecos

Alan C. Porter

A Black Horse Western

ROBERT HALE · LONDON

ISBN 0 7090 4694 4

Robert Hale Limited
Clerkenwell House
Clerkenwell Green
London EC1R 0HT

To my wife, Janet,
with love.

Photoset by PRG Graphics
Printed and Bound in Great Britain by WBC Print Ltd, and
WBC Bookbinders Ltd, Bridgend, Glamorgan.

ONE

Pappy Duke was a mean cuss, but his three sons were meaner. In all their years of robbing and killing they made only one mistake. They left Matt Holder alive.

This was not intentional: they expected him to die in the baking Texan desert. After stripping him naked, breaking both arms and pushing cactus thorns deep into the soles of his feet, they left him to die. Matt's eight, coming-on nine-year-old son Ben did not survive.

When the Dukes rode into their desert camp and started beating on his pa, Ben had kicked Rafe Duke in boyish anger. In reply, Rafe Duke had pulled his pistol and shot the boy between the eyes. It was this terrible memory that had kept Matt alive in the days of agony that followed. He had been forced to walk in the burning wilderness until the cactus thorns were pushed flush to the soles of his feet and the hot sun had burned and blistered his naked flesh.

He was found five days later, near to death, by the sisters from the Sisters of Mercy mission and within the cool, white, adobe walls of the mission they had nursed him back to life. Four months later, in the August of 1886, he was ready to leave the protective confines of the mission.

He stood tall and whipcord thin: a man in his late twenties whose lean, bearded face still bore the ravages of grief that put dark hollows beneath his eyes and carved lines into his forehead. Dark hair, shot through on the right-hand side with a stream of silver, tangled long about his ears as he stared down with hard, grey eyes at the tiny grave. Here, in a quiet corner of the walled garden, against a back-cloth of red roses rested the mortal remains of his son Ben.

About a month before he had gone back into the desert to where the wagon lay broken and forgotten, boards shrunken and split beneath the furnace stare of the sun. It was amid the sun-whitened rocks that shimmered in the dry air that he found the tiny, picked-clean bones and returned with them to the mission to give them a decent burial.

'It troubles me that there is so much hatred in your heart, Matthew.' The mother superior in austere black and white stood at his side, a sadness in her gentle, lined face.

'Ben was a good boy. We had plans until a bunch of strangers took his life away. Yes, I have hatred, mother.' Matt turned his eyes on the holy woman, barely suppressed anger in his voice.

She looked into their hard, grey depths and shivered inwardly. The man had survived against impossible odds. She remembered the day he had been brought in, body blistered, arms broken and his feet!

— swollen and festering with the wicked thorns embedded in them. She had not expected him to live. Some inner spark refused to let him die, but at what cost? The eyes that she looked into were dead, soulless chips of grey metal; eyes without compassion or feeling. Though he lived, something had died within him.

'God will punish the sinners,' she pointed out softly, and a pale smile flickered across his bearded lips.

'I'm afraid I can't wait that long,' he replied.

'I will pray for you, Matthew,' she said and again saw the smile.

'I owe you and the sisters more than I can ever repay. I will not forget you. Will you tend Ben's grave for me?'

'He will not be forgotten. But you, Matthew, will you not reconsider? Revenge is an evil path to take. It can destroy the innocent as well as the guilty.'

'I owe Ben,' Matt replied and placed the tan stetson he had been turning in his big hands on his head. The mishmash of clothing he now wore was gathered from oddments the sisters had collected over the years. The dark pants almost fitted, needing an inch or so more length. Likewise the brown jacket: a little short in the sleeves. Only the red check shirt fitted comfortably. The scuffed, tan boots were holed and hurt his feet, but a strip of hide placed inside each boot cured the hole problem as long as it didn't rain. He could do nothing about the hurting except suffer it in silence. 'If'n you can't accept my reasons then please try to understand them.'

'I will try,' she promised. 'Take this.' She thrust twenty dollars into his surprised hands.

'I can't take your money,' he protested.

'It will buy you food and shelter for a few days. We have enough money for our needs. Please take it. A man with no money is more apt to fall by the wayside.'

Matt, embarrassed, slipped the money into a pocket of his pants. 'I'm obliged, mother,' he said.

'Sister Lucy and Sister Beth will take you to the way-station in the wagon. From there the Pecos stage will take you to Larkinsville. Look out Seth Coggins at the livery stable. He is always in need of hostlers. God be with you, Matthew Holder.'

The way-station was a ramshackle affair of sun-warped boards and peeling paint. At one time it had stood proud at the side of the desert road with its white walls and red roof. Now it exuded an air of neglect as its red and white paint only clung in a few, stubborn places. Next to it lay a spindly fenced corral and a dilapidated barn.

The interior of the way-station matched the exterior. A small bar stretched along half the back wall while the centre-piece of the room was a long, wooden trestle-table, scarred and stained and accompanied on either side by long benches. The place smelt of sweat and smoke and flies gathered about congealed globules of something that littered the floor around the table. The man behind the bar, wearing a sweat-stained vest and a good three-days growth of beard, offered Matt the choice between yesterday's beans hotted up or a glass of whiskey. Matt chose the latter and with a stogie to accompany it returned outside to the shade of the veranda and settled himself in a creaking rocker to drink, smoke and wait for the stage. The whiskey and cigar tasted good after four months of abstinence.

The stage from Pecos jangled and clattered in an hour later, trailing a wake of brown dust. Its maroon and yellow coachwork was barely visible beneath a thick coating of dust and grime. Matt watched as driver and guard climbed stiffly down.

'Larkinsville?' A head poked from the door window.

'Desert Fork way-station, mister. We move ag'in in an hour. You can get a bite to eat here, but I wouldn't recommend it if'n you wanna stay alive,' the driver said laconically.

The words brought a smile to Matt's face as an old Mexican hobbled from the stable by the corral to feed and water the horses.

The stage left on time and, apart from Matt, the only other traveller was a drummer from Pecos in a grubby white suit and black derby and a big, green-stoned ring on one fat finger. His reaction on entering the way-station was to leave even quicker, a hand to his mouth, muttering, 'My oh my', over and over again.

They had been travelling a little over an hour when gunshots from outside brought the dozing Matt fully awake. He was thrown forward as the stage slithered to a halt.

'What's happening?' the drummer demanded as

Matt picked himself up from a kneeling position on the floor, swearing softly.

'You folks inside, step out 'less'n you wanna be carried out feet first.' To accompany the roughly spoken words the door on Matt's side was jerked open and a masked figure pointed a gun in.

'It's a hold-up,' the drummer squealed unnecessarily, face turning dough-white.

'Look lively, folks, as we're plumb low on patience and if'n you're packing iron, toss it out real gentle-like.'

There were two of them, the second sitting astride a big roan with a pistol pointed at the guard while the driver stared stolidly ahead. They were both young, faces hidden behind colourful bandannas and low hat brims. Both wore nondescript working clothes, but the boots of the one standing looked expensive.

'We're collecting for a good cause folks — us — so please give generously.' The rider giggled at his partner's inane joke. A small gunny-sack was held open before Matt and the Navy Colt aimed at a spot midway between his eyes as an inducement to comply. Matt saw no sense getting killed for the remaining twelve dollars of his money.

'Is that all you got, pilgrim?' The robber eyed Matt suspiciously, running his eyes over his ill-fitting clothes. 'I guess it is. Did you rob someone to get that much?' He chuckled at his joke.

He did much better with the quaking drummer: a hundred dollars and the drummer's ring. Finally the robber mounted a waiting horse.

'Been a pure pleasure doing business with you

folks,' he called and, with his partner, turned and galloped off.

'This is an outrage,' the drummer stormed.

'You're still alive, aren't you?' Matt said dryly and looked up at the driver and guard. 'Get much of this, do you?'

'One of the hazards of stage travel,' the driver replied. 'Climb aboard, folks. Won't do to arrive in town late.'

Five hours later the stage rolled into Larkinsville and Matt slipped silently away while the drummer regaled a curious few with tales of the hold-up.

Larkinsville was no different to any other small, western town. A series of clapboard and adobe buildings straddling a wide, dusty main-street. Matt had seen the livery stable on the way in and now headed for it. The warm interior smelt of hay and horse droppings. A few horses in tumbledown stalls whickered as he passed by. There was no one about so he headed for the open doors at the far end. These led into a square corral where an old man and a girl groomed a pair of horses.

Matt paused in the entrance and called, 'I'm looking for a Seth Coggins.'

The old man ceased his grooming and peered across at Matt.

'You're looking at him, stranger. What can I be doing for you?'

'The Sisters of Mercy said you might have a job going. The name's Holder, Matt Holder.'

The old man limped forward and extended a gnarled hand. What little hair he did have lay whitely about his ears.

'Heared about you. Found in the desert near to death, so they say.'

'They say right,' Matt agreed.

'Know about horses?'

'Some,' Matt replied.

'Some sounds just about right. I kin give a dollar a day. You eat with us and you kin sleep in the hayloft.'

'Sounds good.'

The old man smiled and half turned.

'Hey, Clara, c'mon meet the new hand.'

The girl came shyly across. She looked to be in her late teens, corn-coloured hair pulled back into a single pony-tail. She wiped away a sheen of sweat that was glistening on her forehead.

'Pleased to meet you, ma'am,' Matt responded and the girl giggled.

'Mah granddaughter. Her mah ran off with a drummer after her pa died, so we's look after each other. She ain't got much up top, but she cooks real fine. Well, if'n you're fixing to start, then the stable needs cleaning out and Frank and Curly'll be bringing the stage in soon. Say, you came in on the stage: any trouble?'

Matt told him of the hold-up.

'Well, I'll be.' Seth scratched at his bulbous nose. 'Been a whole spate of robberies lately and not only the stage. The general store got busted a couple o' weeks back. Luke Ramsey had his ranch broken into. The whole world's gone mad.'

'Must be the lawless times we live in,' Matt

grunted.

Later that evening as the sun slid away to the west and the night shadows crawled over Larkinsville, wrapping it in a cocoon of velvety darkness, Matt joined Seth and Clara for supper. Matt had to admit to himself that he was more than a mite peckish. The stable had not been properly cleaned out for quite a spell, so he had worked himself up a real appetite. As Clara ladled generous portions of beef stew and dumplings onto a plate before him, the smell told Matt that Seth's claims to Clara's cooking had not been an empty brag and tasting the stew proved it. Matt had two good helpings before reluctantly refusing any more.

'Sure sorry you wuz robbed, Matt,' Seth said as he fetched out a pipe.

'Don't pay it no mind,' Matt replied lazily.

'Reckon it's local kids playing at outlaw,' Seth mused as Clara cleared away the plates. 'One thing's for sure they ain't the Dukes. They kill first. Happen you met 'em in the desert, Matt?' He eyed Matt.

'Happen I did,' Matt agreed thinly after spooning sugar into his coffee and absently stirring it as dark memories leapt unbidden into his mind.

Pappy Duke, short and stocky, withered with age, clad in a black frock-coat and stovepipe hat. He looked a cross between a preacher and a lawyer, but all he preached was death and the only law he knew was that of the gun.

Rafe Duke, a big, hulking brute of a man built like a canyon wall and twice as hard. His eyes bulged and his wide mouth was full of yellow, crooked teeth when he smiled, and he smiled a lot when he was killing.

That left Billy. Blond-haired and blue-eyed with a smooth-skinned handsomeness that had quickened many a girl's heart. Billy was the gunman, the fast draw of the four with a liking for expensive clothes. And finally there was Jack. He did the cooking and the cleaning, looked after the horses. Giggled a lot and stank even more. He was heavy and overweight for his size, the top of his head coming just level with Matt's shoulder. He liked to do things with the big, broad-bladed knife he carried. These things were only spoken of by the others and had made his blood run cold.

'You were lucky to survive, son, from what I heared,' Seth added, pulling on the pipe.

'So they tell me. How come the Dukes haven't been hunted down and put out of business yet?'

'Ain't for the want of trying. A lot of men have tried and they ain't ever come back. There's $10,000 apiece on them, dead or alive. $40,000 riding free that no one's been able to collect. I guess no one tries now. They're one mean family. Even the Apaches steer clear of the Dukes. Reckon them boys plumb came straight from hell. They just appear. Mebbe don't hear about them for months, then they're back, killing and robbing. Raping women and girl-children alike.' He snorted his disgust. 'Reckon they gota hideout in the canyon country west of Desert Springs, but that's mighty wild country. News is you had a boy with you when the Dukes rode in.' He flicked a bright eye on Matt, the smoke from his pipe curling about the hanging oil lamp.

'News gets about,' Matt commented.

'And nothing gets about faster'n bad news,' Seth replied. His eyes were still on Matt and he saw the sudden flare of grief that filled the grey eyes for a second only to be washed away and replaced by rage: a dark rage that sculpted the bearded face with grim, hard lines. 'Say, son, I'm sorry if'n I stirred bad memories,' Seth continued quickly, but Matt appeared not to hear him. His eyes stared at a knot in the wooden surface of the table.

'He was my son Ben. Eight years old. Would have been nine now but for them.' There was a brief, bitter smile that became a scowl. 'He tried to stand up for his pa so they killed him. The big one called Rafe put the bullet between his eyes and laughed when he did it.' Matt's hands clenched on the table-top. 'It's something I won't ever be forgetting. The Dukes made one big mistake when they rode away that day.' His eyes locked with Seth's.

'What's that son?' Seth asked nervously.

'They left me alive,' Matt replied bleakly.

TWO

It was three days later that trouble found its way to Matt. He had been busy repairing the stalls in the livery stable when he heard a commotion from outside.

'Leave her alone, yer varmint,' Seth's voice raved on the hot air. His words were followed by coarse, ribald laughter and Clara calling out in a frightened voice, 'Grandpa!'

Matt moved to the double doors that lay open to the corral. To the right Seth and Clara had been backed into a corner where fence and stable joined. Seth stood protectively before Clara, facing two young cowboys.

'Get out of the way, old man. It's about time Clara here had a taste of what a man's got to offer.' The speaker, blond-haired and dressed in expensive range clothes and hand-made boots, grabbed the front of his pants suggestively. 'How about it, Clara? Step outta your drawers and I'll give you a bitta prime beef.'

'You dirty-mouthed scum,' Seth shouted. 'I'll tell yer grandpa and he'll wup you fer sure . . . ah!' The last cry was forced from the old man's lips as a hand slapped hard against the side of his face spinning him against the side of the stable. The next second the young cowboy moved roughly in on the dazed old man. He spun him around, grabbed a double handful of shirt-front and rammed him hard against the stable wall, holding him there.

'You best keep your mouth shut, old man, if'n you know what's good for you. Accidents happen 'round a place like this. Mebbe you could fall on a hayfork or a sudden fire . . . '

'Don't you hurt grandpa none,' Clara stormed, shrinking back into the corner.

'We ain't gonne hurt him, girl. No, we's gonna let him sit and watch as we make a woman outta you.'

With growing anger, and aware that they were armed and he was not, Matt stepped clear of the doorway.

'It would take a man to do that, not a boy,' he called.

They both turned guiltily at the voice, blondie releasing the old man and stepping back. Matt had removed his shirt while working in the stable and the two found themselves looking at a lean, muscular figure with a tangle of dark hair across his chest. Blondie had been careful not to make a play for his pistol, but now, seeing the man was unarmed, he settled his hand ominously over the pearl handle. Matt noted the move as he bent to help Seth up from his knees.

'Pulling that gun would be a real foolish thing to do, boy. I'm not armed and that would be murder in front of witnesses.'

Blondie looked undecided until the second youngster laid a hand on his arm. 'He's right, Tom.'

Tom shook the restraining hand away.

'So you've got yourself some hired help, old man,' he sneered.

'Ain't that just right, Tom Larkins.' It was the old man's turn to sneer.

'Well, pilgrim, as you're new around here we'd best acquaint you with a few facts. My grandpa built this town, so if'n you wanna stay around you keep your nose outta what don't concern you.'

Matt's ears had pricked up at the expression pilgrim. He seemed to recall hearing it before — and recently. He studied the youth intently. He was about the right height and hair colouring. Tom Larkins grinned, mistaking Matt's silence for awe, but the grin soon faded as Matt replied, 'Reckon we've met before, boy and then it cost me twelve dollars.'

Tom's jaw dropped and beside him Dan Larkins looked uncomfortable.

'You must be loco,' Tom spluttered thickly and Matt knew he had hit pay-dirt.

'No, just a poor stage traveller that ended up even poorer.'

'What are you saying, pilgrim? That we robbed the stage? That we'uns are nothing but dirty, thieving hold-up-men?' There was forced belligerence in his voice as he sought to bluff the other into doubt.

'Seem to remember one of the robbers called me pilgrim. He had blond hair too,' Matt continued remorselessly.

'Are you calling me a liar, mister?' Tom came off defence and into attack. 'A liar and a thief?'

'The name's Matt Holder and I call what I see. What do you see, Tom Larkins?'

'I see a dead man,' Tom replied flatly. 'You'd better start packing iron, pilgrim. The next time I see you I'll be shooting.'

'The next time I see you I'll expect my twelve dollars back,' Matt replied.

'Figured you for a no account, Tom Larkins,' Seth barked. 'If'n you'd hit an old man and start in on a girl like Clara, you must be pretty low-life. I'll make sure your grandpappy hears what you did and he won't be pleased none.' The old man's eyes gleamed happily in anticipation of his threat.

Tom's eyes flickered contemptuously to the old man and then back to Matt.

'Don't go getting too cocky, old man. This drifter won't be around forever, maybe a lot less time than he thinks. You and me are not finished yet.' He poked a warning finger at Matt. 'I'll be back and you'd better believe it.'

'With my twelve dollars,' Matt goaded.

An expression of fury and hate glided over Tom's face and lingered in his eyes. Without another word he turned and stomped away, followed by his brother Dan.

Seth glanced up at Matt in admiration.

'Son, you were within a whisker of shaking hands with death.'

Matt smiled bleakly.

'I've shook his hand before, Seth and he don't scare me. You all right, Miss Clara?'

Clara looked at the big man shyly and nodded her head dumbly.

'Well it sure scares me,' Seth continued as Clara left the corral and headed for the house. 'The Larkins do just about whatever they damn choose around here. First it was just plain mischief, now they're getting mean. Tom now, he's taking after his pappy and he got hisself shot on main street. Old Abe Larkins looks after them, but his control is slipping now.' He shook his head in sorrow. 'He's getting old and ain't got the grip to keep 'em in line.'

'I take it he's the Larkins that built this place.'

'Yup. Got a big spread to the west of town, the circle L, and one day it'll belong to Tom and Dan.'

'If they live that long. Someday you've gotta match your mouth with some action. There are kids like the Larkins in every town. They either learn a bit of sense quick or die young.'

'Seems like you could be right,' Seth nodded his head. 'You figure them for the stage robbers?'

'And the others you mentioned if I'm thinking right.'

'Ain't that something. Makes sense. No strangers been seen about and they always seem to have money after a robbery. Better watch yourself, Matt, you've made a powerful enemy in the Larkins boys.'

'I'll bear it in mind,' Matt promised and returned to his unfinished work in the stable.

The matter slipped from his mind as the day wore on, but it reared its head again later when the evening sun painted the white walls of the town red. Matt was in the house that lay the other side of the corral when a voice from outside called, 'Come on out, pilgrim. We got some unfinished business and you'd better be packin' iron.'

Seth darted across to the window and Clara looked fearfully up from the cooking range.

'It's the Larkins boys with a bunch of the town yahoos and they ain't looking too friendly,' Seth relayed to Matt worriedly as the big man joined him.

'You called me a thief and a liar, pilgrim. You owe me some real good apologizing or the undertaker's gonna get some business,' Tom shouted and a ripple of laughter ran about the five that backed him. Dan stood a little to his brother's left. The five toted Winchesters and a bottle that they passed around.

'He's got the right, Matt. You did call him those things. I reckon he's got the clout to put a slug in you brains whether you're armed or not and get away with it.'

'I'm calling you out, pilgrim. Here's a gunbelt for you if'n you ain't got your own.' Tom slung a folded gunbelt towards the door. Those inside heard it thud onto the wooden boards outside.

'Kin you use a gun?' Seth asked anxiously.

'Some,' Matt admitted.

'Some ain't good enough, but it'll have to do. Hang on. The one Tom's thrown is just as likely to be unloaded or something.' He darted across the room as he spoke and rummaged in an old chest, set against a side wall. He returned seconds later with a gunbelt. 'Here.' He thrust it into Matt's hands. Matt drew the weapon from its holster. It was a Schofield-Smith and Wesson six shot, cleaned, loaded and well looked after. Matt raised questioning eyes to the old man.

'I used to be a gunsmith afore I took on this place. I still do a bit of work in that direction. That belonged to a customer who never came back for it. I heard later that he caught a dose o' lead poisoning. Careful, the trigger's a mite tetchy. Barrel's an inch longer too. Holster's cut away to accommodate the extra length on a fast draw.'

Matt slide the gun back and buckled the gunbelt on, settling it comfortably on his hip before tying the leg string.

'Are you coming out, pilgrim, or do you want us to burn you out? Livery stable'd go up real fine.'

'Do you know what you're doing, son?' Seth asked anxiously.

Matt smiled, opened the front door and stepped out, walking forward until he was clear of the veranda overhang.

'Glad to see you're packing iron, pilgrim,' Tom began.

'The name's Holder, boy, Matt Holder.' He hooked the thumb of his left hand into the belt by the buckle and let his right hand hang loosely over the butt of the gun. 'See you brought a few friends. Is it you and me, or them and me?'

'I fight my own battles, pilgrim,' Tom said, tight-lipped.

By now wind of what was happening at the livery stable was all over town and people were appearing, grouping at a respectful distance to watch.

'Then best make your play, boy, afore it gets too dark to see,' Matt said softly.

The smile drained from Tom's face and his body became tense. To the west the blood-red sky was veined with glittering gold while to the east a deep purple sky pushed dark shadows ahead of it.

Tom went for his gun. It was half drawn from its holster when he found himself looking down the barrel of Matt's weapon. He froze, hearing shocked gasps from behind, not believing the speed of the man's draw.

The gun in Matt's hand had become an extension of his fully outstretched arm and was pointing un- waveringly between the young man's staring eyes set in a sudden, chalk-white face.

'Your first mistake was in thinking that I was an easy take. Your second was thinking I couldn't handle a gun. Your third mistake would be in pulling that gun. But you make up your own mind. It don't make no difference to me if you end up dead or alive.'

Hooves thundered and harness jangled to Matt's right. From the corner of his eye he saw four riders appear. They came to a slithering halt and an old man in black dismounted, an iron-grey beard de- corating his lower face. He planted himself next to Tom.

'I can't blame you if you finish the job, mister, but I'm bound to tell you that if'n you do you'll end up as dead as him. He's kin, I'm sorry to say; but you gotta stand by kin.'

The three mounted men were hard rangemen. With their backs to the sunset only their eyes glimmered in the pale oval of their faces.

Matt released the hammer and lowered the weapon, returning it to its holster, but keeping his hand on the butt.

'I'm beholding to you, mister,' the old man said.

'He threatened to kill us, Grandpa . . . ' Tom began and the old man rounded on him and struck him across the mouth with his hand. The blow sent the younger man staggering back into his brother. Anger spat from the old man's eyes.

'I heard what you were up to, boy, and prayed that I'd be on time. You're just like your pa and that ain't nothing to be proud of because he's dead. Shot like you could have been. Now get out of my sight.' He looked to the rangemen. 'Make sure they get home safe and sound, Tate. I ain't finished with them yet. I'll be along directly.'

'OK, Mr Larkins.' By now the layabouts that had accompanied Tom and his brother had melted into the background. Abe Larkins turned back to Matt.

'I don't know your name, stranger.'

'Matt Holder.'

'I'm obliged to you for letting the boy live. You must be pretty fast to have got the drop on Tom.'

'Fast . . . fast . . . ' By now Seth had tumbled from the house. 'I ain't never see'd a gun drawn like that afore.' There was admiration and awe in Seth's voice.

'I didn't want to kill your grandson, Mr Larkins, but someone will someday if he carries on the way he is.'

'I can't watch him all the time. Was a time when they'd do as I say, but now . . . ' he shrugged his shoulders. 'They're between being boys and men. I can't handle 'em like I used to. Tom is headstrong, like his pa. He'll be looking for revenge. You shamed him in front of his friends.'

'Then next time he might not be so lucky,' Matt pointed out. 'I'm sorry to say that it was your grandsons that have been robbing the stage and the local ranchers.'

Abe Larkins seemed to wilt at the news. He drew himself up. 'We've only your word for that, Holder,' he said stiffly.

'Look out the drummer that came in on the stage a few days ago. Ask him about the ring that was taken and the one that Tom's been wearing. I haven't got no axe to grind, Mr Larkins, against the boys. It's all of their own doing.'

'What will it take to get you to leave town, Mr Holder?'

'I don't accept pay-offs,' Matt said bluntly. 'As soon as I get a stake I'll be gone, got revenge of my own to take care of.'

'$500 and it's no pay-off. I'm just trying to keep my grandsons alive. Look on it as the stake you're after. Leave by first light and it's yours.' Abe produced a pocket-book and from it extracted a wad of notes. Matt eyed the wad.

'The Dukes left me in the desert to die and that was after killing my boy, Ben. Just eight years old, coming on nine, and they killed him. I'll take your money, Mr Larkins, just as long as you remember I'm not running from town. I owe a boy that never had the chance to reach manhood and that's why I'm taking the money. Teach your grandsons some respect, Mr Larkins, or you'll end up as lonely and hurting as me.'

'I'll bear it in mind, Mr Holder. I wish you luck in going after the Dukes. A lot have tried an' they're all dead.'

'I'll keep it in mind,' Matt said.

'How'd you learn to use a gun like that?' Seth asked as Abe Larkins mounted his horse and kneed it towards the sunset.

'It's easy to learn, Seth. It's the unlearning that comes a mite hard.'

'Eh?' Seth scratched his head.

'I spent five years in Yuma unlearning,' Matt replied. 'I used to be like Tom Larkins, always on the lookout to prove myself. I killed a man in a shoot-out. It was a fair enough fight, but the judge didn't cotton to gunslingers and I ended up in Yuma. My wife couldn't stand the shame. She ran off with another man and left Ben in the care of an old widder-woman. When I came out I swore I'd never touch a gun again. I collected Ben, worked to build up a stake then headed out here for a new life. Running into the Dukes put an end to that. You can't escape your destiny, Seth.' Matt shook his head regretfully. 'If'n I hadn't learned to use a gun. I wouldn't have ended up in Yuma. I'd still have a wife and Ben would be alive today. Now all I've got is memories and a hurt that only a gun can cure. I guess

I've come full circle the hard way.'

'It can be a fatal cure, Matt,' Seth pointed out. 'The Dukes are bad medicine. They don't die easy.'

'Neither do I, Seth,' Matt replied softly. 'Neither do I.'

THREE

It was four days later that Matt rode into Desert
Springs clad in blue Levis, and blue cotton shirt, a
light tan buckskin jacket with matching boots and
hat and a yellow bandanna at his throat. Seth had
insisted he keep the Schofield-Smith and Wesson
and had refused payment for a fine bay stallion, but
Matt had left a hundred dollars in the livery stable
for the old man to find.

Since leaving Larkinsville Matt had stopped off at
Fort Stockton to buy the clothes he now wore and
add a Winchester to his arsenal. It was there he
heard again that the Dukes had a hideout somewhere in the maze of canyons and desert flats that
ran along the base of the Davis Mountains – a wild,
untamed region of sand, stone, scrub, cactus and
Apaches that lay west of Desert Springs.

'Mountain Bend's where the Dukes are most likely
to hang out,' a garrulous barber informed him. 'And
that's one hell-place that decent folk stay well clear
of.' The barber had been full of tales about the
Dukes. Moans and groans about the inability of the
law to catch them and what he'd like to do to them if
he was ever in a position to catch them. In the end

Matt was sorry he had ever raised the question of the Dukes.

By now it was getting late. After bedding his horse down at the livery stable Matt took himself a room at the hotel for the night.

As for Tom and Dan Larkins, they spent a less-than-comfortable night with sand and rock for a mattress. Tom, shamed by the way Matt Holder had outdrawn him, was looking for revenge. Old man Larkins had been real sore at them, cussed them from one end of the house to the other. If that wasn't bad enough, news that they were the stage robbers had spread like wildfire through the town and various irate officials came knocking at the door the following morning. People were putting two and two together and coming up with the right answer that the two were also responsible for the local break-ins.

In order to defuse the situation Abe Larkins found it necessary to pay out large sums of money. As a result of which Abe Larkins sent the two away from the ranch to spend a week or so on the South Ridge, riding line and spending long nights in a cold, cheerless, uncomfortable shack. It was this prospect that did not sit well with Tom. He liked the comforts of whiskey and women. After three days of spartan existence in the draughty line-shack, Tom had an idea and after talking out his idea with Dan, the two left the line-shack and headed west. Before they bedded down for the night, Dan began voicing doubts.

'I don't like it, Tom,' he moaned for the hundredth time. He sat, with a blanket wrapped about his shoulders to keep the desert cold out, before a small, flickering fire. The flames reddened his face and sent shadows dancing nervously into the darkness beyond.

'Goddamit, Dan, will you shut it? Matt Holder near got us strung up and I for one ain't letting him get away with it.' Tom's eyes gleamed darkly in the vicious set of his face.

'But going looking for the Dukes . . . ' Dan objected.

'We'll be doing them a favour and ourselves.'

'You reckon so?'

'I know so.' Tom tossed a stick into the flames. 'They'll be beholding to us for telling them that Holder is gunning for them and when Holder turns up they'll be waiting for him. Look, I got a few bits and pieces we took from the Hoskins ranch. We pay the Dukes to put them on Holder's body and dump it outside of town, then when it's found the townsfolk are gonna think that Holder was the robber. He'll be dead so he won't be able to answer any questions, and we come out of it innocent. I brung along five hundred bucks to pay the Dukes for their services. It's a cinch, boy.' Tom grinned and rubbed his hands.

'How'll we find the Dukes? Tell me that.'

'That's my little surprise. I know where their hideout is.'

Dan's head snapped up and he looked across at his grinning brother.

'Now how can you know that?'

''member that renegade 'pache that me and the

boys tracked into canyon country a summer back? Smokey and I, after we split up, came across this old trapper's cabin with horses tied up outside. We stayed in the rocks keeping watch and who should come out of it but the Dukes.'

'And you didn't tell anyone?'

'Figured it might come in useful one day and it has. That's another reason the Dukes will have for thanking me.'

'I hope you're right.' Dan was not convinced.

'Quit worrying, brother, it's in the bag. We make contact with the Dukes at first light, do our little bit o' horse trading then head back to the line-shack and wait. Now get some sleep.'

It was around mid-morning of the following day that the pair reined their mounts to stop. Ahead of them and to the right stood the log cabin that Tom had spoken of. On three sides rock walls climbed sheer to the sky. The third side was open on to a steep depression chocked with stunted, tangled thorn-bushes, its stony sides clothed in brown, dead grass.

'So what do we do now?' Dan whispered. There was a tiny corral next to the tumbledown cabin where four horses were housed.

'Best let 'em know we're here afore they get itchy fingers.' Tom stood up in the saddle causing leather to creak and cupped his hands about his mouth ready to holler their presence.

'You'd better have a good reason for being here, boys,' a quiet voice said from behind, and was followed by the metallic cocking of a rifle. The horses shied a little at the sudden voice.

'We ain't looking for no trouble, mister,' Tom said quickly as he brought his horse under control and found himself looking down into the smiling, handsome face of Billy Duke.

'Well you've found it, boy,' Billy replied ominously. 'Creeping up on folk . . . .'

'You've got it wrong.' Tom raised his hands. 'We're here to see Pappy Duke. We've got a bit of news that he'd be right pleased to hear and the chance to make some money, real easy-like. Ain't that so, Dan?' Dan's head bobbled vigorously.

Billy eyed them.

'Hey, pa. We got ourselves some company,' he yelled and the cabin door opened.

'We already had the drop on 'em.' Pappy Duke emerged, followed by the hulking Rafe and the fat Jack. 'Just fixing to blow their heads off when you showed up.' Pappy marched to within a few yards of the two and the scowl on his face turned to an amiable grin. 'Don't get many callers. It's right neighbourly of you boys to drop by. How did you know where we were?' Tom filled him in on the events that led up to the accidental discovery of the hideout and afterwards Pappy said, 'And you never told no one?'

'No, sir.'

'How's about this Smokey fella?'

'Got hisself stomped to death in a stampede six months ago.'

'Ain't that a pure shame?' Pappy shook his head dolefully.

'Reckon they got important noos, pa,' Billy informed.

'Ain't that purely somethin'?' Pappy breathed, eyes wide.

'Sure is, pa,' Rafe agreed, his bulging, watery eyes taking in the two.

'Kin I cut them a little, pa?' Jack asked hopefully, a large hunting knife appearing suddenly in one fat, grubby hand.

'Now you cut that out, Jack,' Pappy admonished, grinning.

'Figure that's what he wants to do, pa,' Billy sang out.

'I'm getting plumb outta practice.' Jack moaned his disappointment.

'Now hush that talk, Jack, or folks'll get the wrong impression. Step down boys afore I bust my neck looking up at you and you can tell us what brung you all this way.' Both boys hesitated, eyes on Jack and the knife he caressed in his fat, grimy hands. Pappy saw the direction in which they were looking. 'Pay no mind to Jack, boys. He was just fooling. Weren't you, Jack?'

'Just fooling, pa,' Jack agreed and giggled.

With hesitation, the two dismounted and the four closed in around them. Rafe led the horses away before they could protest and tied them to a hitching post. Both boys felt suddenly very vulnerable. Tom forced himself to relax.

'Who are you, boys?'

'Tom and Dan Larkins, I'm Tom. Our grandpappy built Larkinsville.'

'You must be mighty important dudes then.'

'Some,' Tom agreed importantly.

'So what noos brings you here?' Pappy asked.

'Truth is, there's a real mean gunslick gunning for you and your boys. He was in Larkinsville a few days ago, but he's gone now, out looking for you I guess.'

'Does he know about this place?'

'Nobody knows but us,' Tom promised.

'Who is this man?' Billy demanded.

'Name of Holder, Matt Holder, and he can pull a gun faster'n greased lightning.' As Billy scowled at that Matt added to Pappy's face, 'I ain't no slouch at that fast draw, but he beat me.'

'Never heard of him,' Pappy said. 'Any of you boys run across a Matt Holder?' There was a chorus of noes.

'Seems you and your boys killed his boy and left him to die in the desert some four, five months ago over Desert Rock way. Bunch of sisters that run a mission there found him and nursed him back to health. Seems he don't want nothing more than to kill all of you.'

'Reckon I kin remember a man and a boy 'bout the time you say.' He squinted at Tom. 'Why you boys so worried 'bout what happens to us?'

'He caused us a whole heap of trouble before he left Larkinsville and we aim to pay him back and clear our name.'

'How you gonna do that, boy?'

'I got $500 for you to kill Holder and put some articles I'll give you on his body and leave him just outside town.'

Pappy looked thoughtful.

'What you boys been up to?'

'Just relieving a few stage travellers of their valuables.' Tom smirked as he said it. 'Only, this Holder recognized us and started making accusations, so we lit out and come to you to help us with our little problem.'

'Stage robbers, aye. Ain't that illegal, pa?' Billy said.

'Sure sounds that way,' Pappy agreed. 'Five hundred dollars. You brung it with you?'

'Ain't no good mouthing off if'n you can't put up.'

'That's mah way of thinking too,' Pappy said happily. He peered at Dan. 'You don't say much, boy.'

'Tom talks for both of us,' Dan said nervously.

'Can we do business?' Tom asked. He felt at ease now and on top of the situation.

'This fella's fast with a gun you say?'

'Lightning,' Tom agreed.

'Billy here's pretty fast.'

'He'd sure have to be to beat this fella.'

'What say we have a little contest,' Pappy said slyly. 'You agin Billy. See if'n you can get the drop on Billy and you can tell us if'n he's faster than Billy.'

Billy grinned at Tom.

'Got the balls for it, boy?' he goaded.

'Just a contest?' Tom asked.

'Real friendly-like,' Pappy said.

'OK.'

'Tom, don't.' Dan grabbed his arm, alarm in his eyes, but Tom shook it off.

'Should be fun.'

'That's the truth,' Pappy said. 'Move back boys and give 'em room.'

Tom and Billy faced each other.

'Any time you're ready,' Billy called.

Tom's Colt was clear of the holster when a bullet from Billy's .45 took him between the eyes and exited through the back of his head in a shower of blood, bone and brain. Dan stared in horror as Tom's twitching body slammed to the ground.

Pappy moved across to the still body.

'What I plumb forgot to mention was that Billy don't draw his gun less'n he's gonna use it.' He grinned sardonically, then lifted cold, merciless eyes to the white-faced, trembling Dan. The others too were looking at him, Jack thumbing the keen edge of his knife.

FOUR

With a cry of terror Dan turned and plunged down into the rock bowl, heedless of the thorn-bushes that tore spitefully at his clothes and flesh alike.

'Lookee at that boy run,' Rafe shouted, his rat-trap of a mouth grinning broadly to display his big, crooked teeth.

'Are we letting him get away, pa?' Jack asked anxiously as no one made a move to follow.

Pappy Duke massaged his nose and frowned from beneath the tall hat, eyebrows knitting into a single, hairy line.

'Don't figure he's going anywhere.' He eyed the slope the other side of the rock bowl. 'Get the rifles, boys, we's gonna get some target practice.'

Dan heard the whoops of joy that followed Pappy's statement as he crashed through the thorn thickets. Thinking they were following he pushed himself even harder. Panic drove him on. His clothes were ripped and stained with blood from his torn flesh. Tears of pain and fear blurred his vision and he had to wipe them away with a shaking hand.

He broke free of the thorn thickets, risking a quick

glance over his shoulder as he raced low across the bottom of the rock bowl. There was no sign of the Dukes. It puzzled him, but he did not dwell on the fact, for he was too busy trying to stay alive.

He was scrambling up the far side of the rock bowl, feet slipping and sliding on the scree that was loosely held together by the roots of the withered grass, when the first bullet kicked dust to his left. Dan dived to the right and squirmed around to squint back in the direction of the shot. The four Dukes stood against the skyline along the edge of the rock bowl. Now he knew why they had not made any effort to follow him. He was out in the open and they could pick him off on this slope. As Billy raised his rifle, Dan hauled himself up and began a zigzag scramble up the treacherous slope, heart hammering, chest heaving.

The second bullet caught him high on the left shoulder, slamming him down onto the steeply sloping surface, and he had to dig fingers in to stop himself from sliding back. The effort caused pain to flare agonizingly through his damaged shoulder.

'I winged him, pa!' Billy yelled gleefully.

Rafe took the next shot as Dan hauled himself up, but the bullet flew wide of the mark, causing Billy and Jack much loud amusement.

'Hell, boys. You don't get much better as you get older do you?' Pappy grumbled. 'Jack, down on your knees, I need a bit o' support.' Pappy lifted his long-barrelled Sharps Buffalo gun and pulled back the hammer.

'Do I have to, pa? That thing gives me a

headache.'

'Do as I say, boy or I'll wup you good, big as you are.'

'Yes, Pa,' Jack said miserably but did as Pappy bid.

With Jack on his knees and the long barrel resting on his flabby right shoulder, Pappy sighed down the barrel at the small figure scrambling near to the far rim of the bowl. Dan was almost at the top.

The thunderous roar of the Sharps was the last thing Dan heard. The heavy bullet caught him between the shoulder blades and blew half his chest away on the way out. The force of the bullet cartwheeled Dan in a spray of red and sprawled him on his back on top of the ridge, eyes staring sightlessly into the burning sun.

'Right between the shoulders, pa,' Jack exclaimed and gave a cry of anguish as Pappy slapped him in the ear. 'What was that fer?' Jack wobbled to his feet, clutching his ear, while the other two smirked on.

'You musta' moved. I was aiming fer his head.'

Matt came across the Indian twenty miles north of where Tom and Dan had been murdered by the Dukes that very day. The midday sun beat down remorselessly, raising shimmering heat-ghosts from the surrounding rocks and turning scrub thickets brown and lifeless.

He had left Desert Springs at first light and was now deep in the harsh, unremitting terrain between the Davis Mountains in the west and the Pecos River in the east. He had ridden quickly through the coolness of the early morning, now he let the bay select its own pace through the searing, arid wilderness of saguaro cactus and dry scrub.

Apaches had been seen fifty miles south of here and he had been told to keep a wary eye out. It was one problem he did not consider as a problem to worry him, he was not going that far south. Soon he expected to pick up the old stage trail that led over the mountains to El Paso and Mountain Bend waystation. All around him the rocks rose huge and jumbled from the sand and scrub. Great slabs that might have formed part of the foothills once, but time and weather had reduced them to their present state. As he kneed the bay between two huge slabs the animal snorted and shied, ears flattening back. Its actions caused the heat-dozing Matt to jerk awake and his eyes widened as he saw the source of the bay's unease.

The Indian was spreadeagled upright against a great, ragged tooth of rock that reared out of the sand. Ropes came down from the upper edge of the rock and, fastened to his wrists, pulled his brown arms out sideways and up in windmill fashion, and held them there. Likewise ropes attached to his ankles were anchored to thick, wooden stakes holding his legs apart. His feet were off the ground so the weight was on his arms and shoulders. The Indian, an Apache, judging by his long, black hair, had been stripped naked and tortured.

Metal fish-hooks had been pushed through the flesh of the chest and legs and attached to them, by lengths of twine, were heavy rocks that pulled the flesh out in bloody, fly-covered mounds. But by far the worst were the two hooks that had been cruelly pushed through the Apache's scrotum to stretch and tear the delicate sac.

Matt's mouth was dry and his heart thumped as he slid from the saddle and approached the still figure. The Apache's head hung down, his agony-tormented face hidden behind his hair. The flies lifted angrily from the body as Matt approached. Dried blood networked the muscular, brown body in gruesome threads.

'Hell, boy. Somebody sure did the business on you,' he said out loud to himself. 'Ain't no way to die, and that's for sure.' As he looked, sickened at the mutilated sight, the Apache's head lifted and a groan escaped from his cracked lips. Matt jumped as the man's eyes flickered open and stared with dull hate down at him. Matt felt as though he was looking at a corpse that had come alive. The shock froze him for a few seconds, then he reached for the knife in his belt.

The Apache stiffened as he saw the knife appear in Matt's hand, the slight movement causing the suspended rocks to clink together like a gambler's dice. A howl of anguish was torn from his lips as pain carved deep lines into his high cheek-boned face. Blood welled anew from around the hooks.

'Hold still, boy. I'm not about to kill you,' Matt said as he approached nearer to the man, not knowing if he could understand. 'I'll help you if'n I can.'

One at a time, he took the weight of the rocks

hanging from the Apache's scrotum and severed the twine. He removed those from the legs next and finally the chest, all the time being attacked by the flies, angry at being disturbed. Careful as he was, the removal of each rock sent shards of white pain lancing through the Apache's body, which now ran with the sweat of pain.

'I don't know who did this to you, but they've sure got one hell of a mean streak,' Matt said as he tossed the last rock down and stepped back.

'White men!' The words broke in a dry gasp from his lips.

'You speak our tongue!' Matt showed surprise.

'Enough,' the Apache replied.

'What did you do?' Matt asked.

'The Dukes do not need a reason,' came the surprising reply.

'I'm gonna cut you free . . . what do they call you?'

'Red Cloud.'

'Well I'm gonna cut you free, Red Cloud. I'll do the legs first. OK?' Red Cloud nodded and watched as Matt carefully slashed the ropes and eased the Indian's legs together until the bloodless feet touched the ground and the man was able to take the weight from his arms. It must have caused Red Cloud considerable agony, but he made no sound.

'What do they call you, white eyes?' Red Cloud asked painfully.

'Matt Holder.'

'Why do you help me? The white man has no love for the Apache.'

'I've got nothing against the Apache, son. I take each man as I find him. Red or white, there's good and bad in each. Now the Dukes, there's no good in any of them. I'm going up to cut the arm ropes.' Minutes later Matt had scaled the rock and slashed the ropes. When he clambered down, Red Cloud sat with his back to the rock, legs thrust out stiffly before him. Matt fetched his canteen and dribbled water into the Apache's mouth.

'Don't figure you should get too comfortable, Red Cloud. Those hooks have to got to come out afore the blood gets poisoned.'

Red Cloud digested that piece of information in stoic silence, eyes on Matt as he went across to his horse, ferreted in the saddle bags and returned with a small pair of wire cutters.

'How long were you strung up here?'

'One full passing of the sun and stars.' The feeling had returned to Red Cloud's limbs now and he suffered the agony of muscle cramps as the blood flowed unrestricted to hands and feet. Matt fed him some more water.

'That's a fair spell. Now hold still.' Matt started on the chest hooks. 'I'm gonna cut the eyes off the end and then pull the hook all the way through. It's gonna hurt some.'

'Begin, Matt Holder,' Red Cloud said brusquely and stiffened as Matt snipped the ends away. His fingers shook as he pulled the first hook free. The flesh that had swollen about the hook pulled as he dragged the hook free. It must have caused Red Cloud intense pain, but the Indian refused to cry out.

Matt worked as quickly and gently as he could, but blood oozed and trickled from each place, mingling with pain-sweat that once again bathed the Indian's body. Matt was sweating as much, as the hot sun beat down on his back. Finally only the two in the Apache's swollen scrotum remained. Matt took a breather.

'Two more to go. How you doing, Red Cloud?'

'OK, Matt Holder.'

'Then let's finish up.' Matt licked his lips and snipped the ends from the last two hooks, then gripped the Apache's scotum. 'Don't take this as personal,' he joked and then pulled the hooks out.

Red Cloud's face was almost grey as Matt sat back wearily on the hot sand, scooping two handfuls and scouring the blood from his hands.

'Thank you, Matt Holder,' Red Cloud gasped, then his eyes closed and he toppled sideways. An hour later the fever set in on Red Cloud.

Matt had rolled him in a blanket to keep the flies off and when Red Cloud began to moan and twitch Matt found that the Apache was burning up. The man needed a doctor, but they were in short supply around here. He rather doubted that the doctor in Desert Springs would take kindly to doctoring a savage, even if he could get him there. With only one horse between them, Matt knew there was nothing more he could do but wait for the fever to break or Red Cloud to die.

He considered leaving him for his own people to find, but if he was on a lone trip, as it seemed, then there would be no one to find him. In the end his

only choice was to stay with Red Cloud until whatever ends the gods had decreed.

As night fell, Matt lit a fire and prepared himself
for a long, lonely vigil. If there were any of Red
Cloud's friends in the area the fire would attract
them and they would probably kill him on sight. His
morbid thoughts made the night a less than attractive
proposition.

He must have dozed, but suddenly he was wide-
awake without knowing why. The fire had died down
to a red, glowing mound that the darkness was slowly
smothering. Overhead the stars winked and sparkled
in a brilliant cosmic display against the dark, desert
sky. Their brilliance was enough to cast a pale,
ghostly light over the rocks and sand. He sat cross-
legged, shoulders hunched in a blanket that failed to
keep the creeping cold at bay. It rose out of the very
ground and into his bones, stiffening the muscles.

The stillness of the desert was deceptive, filled
with tiny, furtive sounds as nocturnal creatures
awoke and went in search of food. Red Cloud
twitched and moaned in his fever-tormented sleep.

There was movement in a creosote bush to his left;
desert rat maybe? Matt's hand closed on the butt of
the pistol resting in his lap, getting comfort from the
walnut stock as his ears strained and eyes darted
about the misty, silent landscape.

He caught a glimpse of movement from the corner
of one eye, but when he turned his head there was
nothing to see. A night bird flapped overhead setting
his heart thumping. He was getting jumpy. He
looked toward the bay. The animal appeared uncon-

cerned, settled on the ground, legs folded beneath it. If anything or anyone was about, it would have been up and restless. The thought cheered him. He was spooking himself and he smiled as he rose on stiff, creaking joints to ease the cramp from his limbs. Still keeping the blanket about his shoulders, he holstered the pistol and searched out some brushwood to revive the fire. There were still two or three hours to go before daylight; no sense in spending them shivering.

As the brushwood crackled into life he went over and checked on Red Cloud. The Apache's face was sheened in sweat to indicate that the fever still gripped him. Matt returned to the other side of the fire and crouched before it, holding out his hands to the flames.

The first hint of trouble came when the point of a lance pricked the back of his neck.

'Stand, white man,' a guttural voice from behind ordered. As Matt rose slowly to his feet, the blanket slipping from his shoulders, silent figures appeared from all directions and closed in on him. It was only now that the bay whickered and scrambled nervously to its feet. The ring of faces that surrounded Matt were grim and stony-eyed. The metal heads of feathered lances gleamed in the fire glow. Some wore baggy, colourful shirts and hide leggings. Others were bare-chested and barelegged clad in leather breech-cloths. Moccasins shod their feet and colourful headbands kept their long, blue/black hair from their eyes.

Apaches! Matt's skin crawled and his insides tightened.

A hand pulled his gun from its holster as a tall, powerful Apache appeared from the left. He ignored Matt and went straight to Red Cloud. He lifted the blanket and studied the figure for a few minutes before turning to face Matt, eyes bleak in the granite face.

'You did this thing?' his voice broke harshly across the silence.

'I found him strung up on yonder rock. I cut him down.' Matt's voice rasped on a dry throat.

'White eyes do not help Apaches, only kill,' came the accusation.

'I wouldn't be sitting here now if I'd done that,' Matt pointed out. 'He's sick with fever and I couldn't walk away and leave him.'

One of the braves had found the hooks and now held them out silently for the big Apache's examination. There was a mixture of anger and hate in his eyes as he looked at Matt.

'Who did this to Red Cloud?'

'A bunch of low-life characters called Duke.' The sound of the name brought a round of uneasy muttering from the surrounding Apaches. The leader, as Matt presumed him to be, silenced them with a raised hand, and his voice was grave when he spoke.

'We will take Red Cloud back to our village and you will come with us, white eyes.'

'It's the Dukes you want,' Matt protested.

'Until Red Cloud can speak you will remain our prisoner.'

'What if Red Cloud dies?' Matt had a feeling he knew the answer, but required confirmation.

'Then you will die,' came the grim reply.

FIVE

Matt was powerless to do anything. With a sinking heart his hands were bound in front of him, his horse saddled and then his bound hands were tied to the saddlehorn. Their treatment of Red Cloud sent daggers of fear pricking at his heart. The semi-delirious man was tied to a horse and the whole party set off at a fast trot across the desert. Red Cloud moaned and cried out in pain at the start of the journey, but by the time the sun had arisen and progressed across the sky his cries stopped and he lay like one dead, feet tied together beneath the horses belly and hands roped beneath its neck.

The hot morning slid into an equally hot afternoon. Once Matt had tried to talk to the chief.

'We must stop. This will kill Red Cloud.'

With the Apache's stark view of life his reply did little to comfort Matt. 'If that is the will of the Great Spirit then so be it.'

They paused once on the journey and Matt was made to remain in the saddle with the bay's legs hobbled to prevent him getting away. It was mid-afternoon by the time they reached the Apache camp. They had progressed deep into the foothills of the mountains and in a blind canyon, where water fell in a white curtain from the high rocks into a blue pool beneath, lay the Apache camp. It was a collection of semi-permanent, domed huts of hide set in a grove of scrub-oak.

While Red Cloud was carried off to a far hut, Matt became the centre of a group of curious, half-naked children. Young warriors in the transitional period between boyhood and manhood eyed him with open hostility. Matt was cut from his horse and taken away to be tied between two posts, arms outstretched. The need for him to take a leak was denied and in the end he had to relieve himself in his pants, much to the delight of the children who had followed him. They shrieked with unconcealed delight at his humiliation.

He spent an uncomfortable night drifting into light dozes and jerking awake with violent muscle cramps. The following morning an old, leather-faced woman came, gave him water and spoon-fed him a tasteless thick soup. She completed her tasks in silence and went away, leaving him to reflect bitterly on the circumstances that had led to this. If only he had left Red Cloud to die. Instead he had allowed compassion to take over. Because of that compassion and what the Dukes had done to Red Cloud, he was being punished.

All through the long, hot day his misery was increased by the flies. Drawn by the acrid stench of his own urine and sweat they buzzed about his face, settling on his lips and cheeks so that only the most violent shake of his head would dislodge them and then they would return soon after. It was only when night came that he got any relief from their itching attention. His body ached abominably, arms and shoulders especially and it was not until nearly dawn that he finally fell into an exhausted sleep, head forward, held up by the ropes. The sun was well up by the time he jerked awake and found he had company. Some time while he had been asleep a prairie rattlesnake had crawled onto his lap and now lay there comfortably in a series of brown, yellow-striped coils enjoying the warmth of his lap.

Matt's eyes snapped open and the aches and pains were washed away and replaced by fear and revulsion that made his skin crawl and break out in a cold sweat. It was a big son-of-a-bitch too, perhaps five-feet long. Sweat trickled down Matt's nose and dripped onto the scaly body. To Matt's horror the snake moved. It lifted its flat head and turned to probe the droplets of sweat with its darting tongue.

By now word had got around of his predicament and fascinated onlookers began to gather. Braves and squaws, young and old. A child picked up a stone and threw it. It bounced off of Matt's chest and on to the snake's body. Instantly the head with its deadly, soulless eyes reared up and the tail began to rattle. Like dried peas in a can it rattled on, sending Matt's heart into his throat.

The idea of throwing stones caught on with the other youngsters and a hail of stones rained down to agitate the snake even more.

Matt stared at the laughing, jeering crowd. Only one was not laughing with the rest. A young woman.

Midnight-dark hair fell to her shoulders framing an oval, olive-tinted face with large, dark eyes. She stood at the back of the throng and did not laugh. He gave scant thought to why she did not join in the general merriment. The snake was moving angrily on his lap, head reared and waving from side to side as the coils slithered against each other and the rattle from the tail grew louder. Soon it was going to strike out at the nearest object and he was it.

A shadow fell across him and he squinted up. The chief he had not seen since arriving at the Apache village now stood, arms folded across his mighty chest, looking impassively down at him.

'Get this thing off me!' Matt croaked.

'It is the will of the Great Spirit. He sent the snake to test your innocence. If it bites then you are guilty.' With that simple judgement passed, the chief turned and walked away leaving Matt to the caprices of fate. The children, who had ceased their stone throwing upon the chief's arrival, now continued. It seemed to Matt that time had gone into suspension as he waited for the irritated snake to strike. Then, to everyone's disappointment except Matt's, the snake slithered from his lap and wriggled away into the thin undergrowth. Soon after that the crowd dispersed and Matt was left with just the flies for company.

Time passed. The old woman came with food and water. Matt was drifting into a heat-induced doze when a commotion from the direction of the village roused him. Through sun-blurred eyes he saw a group of braves approaching and wondered with cool detachment if this was the end for him. Red Cloud

had died and now it was his turn. He caught the flash
of a knife-blade and steeled himself. He blinked his
watery eyes to clear them and a face swam into view.

'Red Cloud!' The name fell from his parched lips
in a harsh whisper.

Red Cloud, face pale and drawn but eyes clear of
the fever, looked down at Matt.

'I am sorry, my friend,' he said and slashed the
ropes holding Matt's arms. Matt dragged his arms
across his body as they flapped to the ground and
eyed Red Cloud.

'And mighty glad I am to see you,' Matt croaked.

The pool lay to the left of the large one that the
waterfall tumbled into. Lower than its parent, it
picked up the overflow in a bowl-shaped depression
before allowing it to pour back into a tunnel in the
rock. It was here, shaded by a pair of oak, that Matt
now splashed. He had spent the last half an hour in
the pool. His clothes he had washed and were now
draped over hot, sun-kissed rocks to dry, while he
bathed and let the cool water soak into his dry skin.

After Red Cloud had cut him free Matt had been
escorted into the village, given decent food and
water, and finally introduced to the chief by Red
Cloud.

'This is my father, Running Fox. Father, this is
Matt Holder. He saved my life.'

'My son speaks well of you, Matt Holder. You
have proved to be a friend of the Apache. I am glad
my son lived to speak of your friendship.' He extended a big hand and gripped Matt's forearm and

Matt did likewise. 'You are now a friend of the Apache and welcome in our lodges.'

'I'm honoured, Running Fox.' The chief had made no apology for subjecting him to the rough treatment and Matt expected none. The apology came in being accepted as a friend.

'There will be a feast in your honour when darkness falls.'

Matt had wanted to be on his way, but did not want to upset the chief by refusing. He had asked Red Cloud where he could clean himself up and Red Cloud had brought him here and left him. Matt had brought soap from his saddlebags and now, scrubbed from head to foot, he just lazed in the pool while his clothes dried.

He was contemplating getting out when he saw her. She sat on a boulder near the edge of the pool, the young woman with the oval face and the big eyes. She had arrived in silence and her presence startled him.

'Hello,' he called, remembering her presence when the rattler had been on his lap.

'I am called Morning Star,' she said. 'You saved my brother, Red Cloud, when others would have left him to die. Why?' It seemed to Matt that the Indians were having trouble in understanding why a white man should help a red man.

'He needed help, ma'am. Not all white men are like the Dukes.' At the mention of the name she shivered.

'They are demons, not men,' she said fearfully. 'The Apache are afraid of no one. They are fierce

54 *West of the Pecos*

warriors and fighters, but even the bravest are afraid of the Dukes.'

'They're just men, ma'am,' Matt pointed out, casually. 'Mean and murderous men that get pleasure outta killing and hurting, but they can die as easy as any man.'

'You are not afraid of them?' Surprise leapt into her eyes.

'I'm only afraid someone else might kill 'em first and deny me the pleasure.'

'You will go after them?'

'That's what I was doing before I ran into your brother.'

'You are a brave and good man,' she said, serious-eyed and Matt laughed to cover his embarrassment.

'No braver or better than the next,' he shrugged off lightly. 'Now turn your back, Morning Star. I'm about ready to get out of the water.'

'I will help dry you,' she offered.

'You scoot on back to the village. I can dry myself,' he said in alarm.

She suddenly laughed and her whole face lit up.

'I have heard the white men are shy before women. Apache warrior is not afraid.'

'Will you get out of here, Morning Star?' he almost shouted, blushing foolishly.

'Perhaps you have something to be ashamed of?' She cocked an eyebrow mischievously.

Matt splashed water at her with a hand, forcing her to leave the boulder.

'Now git on outta here . . . please.'

Laughing, she darted away.

The promised feast was something well worth waiting for. There was rich meat and tender prairie chicken roasted over open fires and cooked to perfection in their own juices. It was all washed down with a strange milky fluid that was extracted from cactus. It turned out to be mildly alcoholic and by the time the fires were dying down many of the Apaches had fallen into a drunken sleep. Matt was shown a tent by Running Fox and gratefully he threw himself down on to a pile of furs after kicking off boots and socks and tossing his shirt to one side.

He must have fallen asleep, but suddenly he was awake. Moonlight was flooding through the open entrance and glancing across he saw a figure that knelt just within.

Matt blinked the sleep from his eyes and came up on elbows. The figure was Morning Star.

'What are you doing here?' he demanded softly, alarmed at her presence. The last thing he wanted was for Running Fox to appear and discover his daughter here.

'Waiting for you to awaken,' she replied softly, huskily. Before he realized what was happening she lifted her hands to her neck, pulling at the material that clothed her, a robe of some kind, and let it slither from her shoulders to the ground.

Matt caught his breath. The moonlight silvered her full breasts, washed over her naked flesh and put blue fire in her hair.

'Running Fox has given me to you. A gift for saving Red Cloud.'

'Running Fox can't give people as gifts.'

'I am a willing gift,' she replied softly. 'It is the warrior's right to couple with a maiden. You are a great warrior, Matt Holder.'

Matt scrabbled onto his knees and faced her, placing his hands lightly on her shoulders. Now he was closer a subtle, pleasing perfume filled his nostrils. She had rubbed scented oil into her body. Touching her had an electrifying effect on him.

'Haven't you a man of your own to pleasure, Morning Star?'

'You do not like me?' she said sadly.

Matt's body felt hot. His heart was pumping and there was a stiffness at his groin.

'No. I like you Morning Star,' he said hoarsely.

She smiled in the moonlight, took hold of his wrists and guided his hands down on to her breasts. As he felt the hard nipples beneath his palms the last vestiges of resistance fled. He took her in his arms and bore her down on to the bed of furs.

Morning Star knew how to pleasure a man. Matt had known tender love and rough, passionless lust. This was an explosive combination of both as she rode him like an unbroken stallion, then later became the passive seductress beneath his thrusting body. Hardly any words were spoken — none were needed — and when Matt finally fell into an exhausted sleep, she held him close.

Matt awoke with the morning sun streaming in through the open flap. Morning Star was gone. He dressed himself and went outside. Red Cloud called a greeting as he saw Matt and, as Matt crossed to him, his eyes searched the groups of women for

Morning Star.

'You leave today, Matt Holder?'

'I have some unfinished business to attend to that's long overdue,' Matt intoned.

'We eat,' Running Fox boomed. 'A full belly is a comfort on a long journey.'

Matt nodded and again his eyes searched for Morning Star. Running Fox caught the look and smiled.

'She is not here. Do not worry. She is well and happy and will spend one full passing of the sun in prayer to the Great Spirit that the seed within her is fruitful.'

Later, as Matt prepared to leave, Running Fox presented him with a colourful headband that Matt put around his hat crown and was told it was the Band of Friendship.

'All Indians will know you are a friend,' Running Fox explained.

Mounted and ready to go, Matt looked down at Red Cloud.

'You never did tell me what you were doing so far north.'

Red Cloud smiled broadly.

'I was going to steal cattle,' he said.

SIX

Mountain Bend stood on a high, forested plateau of the Davis Mountains. Once it had been a thriving way-station for the stages from El Paso to Pecos, but a new trail had been forged and Mountain Bend forgotten. In its heyday it was an overnight stage stop and a two-storey hotel had been built alongside the way-station and livery stable, to accommodate travellers, and later a general store had appeared and a blacksmiths. All the buildings still remained but they exuded an air of shabby neglect as paint peeled and boards split. At the top of the hotel two of the windows were boarded over, the glass long gone and never replaced. The hotel still had its clientele, but now all it consisted of was gunmen and lawbreakers: the dregs of society.

Mountain Bend was the place to head for if the law was on your tail, for lawmen never ventured into Mountain Bend and Mountain Bend had no law. It had no law-abiding citizens to protect. The closest man to law in Mountain Bend was Josiah Gates. He ran the hotel that was now nothing more than a bawdy house and gambling den.

For Josiah the hotel made him a fat, rich living from the thieves and robbers who came to spend their ill-gotten gains on gambling, women and booze. Money was money and he didn't give a shit where it came from as long as it ended up in his pocket, hence all the means to separate a man from his money: faro, roulette, blackjack, poker and a string of whores.

Just now Gates stood at one end of the long bar and surveyed the fellow that sat in a corner seat down from the grimy windows. Gates was a a fat barrel of a man in a dark suit and a blue silk, ruffle-fronted shirt. His fat, fleshy neck almost swallowed a black bow-tie. His heavy jowls were blue with stubble and small, piggy eyes glared out at the world from beneath the brim of a black stetson. Lank, greasy twists of long dark hair fell from under the stetson and hung untidily about the back of his head. Gates chewed the butt of a cigar as he eyed the stranger. The man had been here for an hour nursing one whiskey and smoking a thin-bodied stogie. He didn't want to gamble or make time with the women and that added up to no profit as far as Gates was concerned and that he didn't like.

Though he gave no indication, Matt was well aware of the other's scrutiny. A man can learn a lot tucked away quietly in a corner and keeping his ears open. It was a trick he had learned in Yuma and it had saved his life on one occasion. For instance, he knew that the fat man observing him was called Josiah Gates and ran the hotel. The fact that he remained in good health and wealth in spite of the rag-bag clientele of killers, thieves and perverts was not down to charisma. Gates had a small army of bully-boys to discourage thievery amongst thieves. Big, hard-eyed men. During the hour he had been sat there, Matt had counted six around the long bar.

Business was brisk. As night came on the poker tables were full. The faro and roulette wheels spun to increase Gate's fortune. No one ever walked out of the hotel with a fistful of winnings, or if they did they did not keep it long, Gates saw to that.

With the ceiling lamps lit, the noise seemed to increase. Matt did not object to the noise. It made people shout to be heard and so he heard also. So far he had not heard anything that he wanted to hear — namely the whereabouts of the Dukes.

Matt sipped at his second whiskey. The half-dozen women were kept busy as a steady stream of traffic went up and down the stairs at one end of the room to a veranda with half a dozen doors leading off that ran above the bar. The opulence that once the hotel had wallowed in could still be seen in the gilt that edged the bar counter and mirror behind.

There was a sudden commotion from the doorway to Matt's left and people scattered, cursing as a figure flew through the batwings and went sprawling on the dusty, dirty boards. It was a negro and when he moved, chains rattled and chinked at ankles and wrists. Matt noticed that the gamblers, having looked around, returned to their games. This was obviously a regular occurrence. Gates was smirking as the negro came to his feet and cowered away as an enormous figure entered. He must have weighed in excess of three hundred pounds. A huge mountain of a man clad in a red tartan jacket, hair tumbling in dark waves to his shoulders. He had a glare that could freeze water.

'Evening, Jake,' Gates greeted.

The boards shook as the mountainous man strode forward to the bar. Nobody stood in his way, nobody was that stupid.

'Gates.' The voice that fell from the man's stubble-ringed lips was nothing more than a harsh whisper.

'Usual, Jake?' the barman enquired and was already splashing whiskey into a glass. The negro was hunkered down at the bar like an animal and Matt felt anger start to burn within him. He still had the scars from ankle irons from his stay in Yuma. The negro's clothes were in tatters and with a feeling of horror he noticed that the man had only three toes on one foot and two on the other. But it was the look in the man's eyes that touched Matt the deepest. A look of utter hopelessness and despair.

Matt noticed then that the gamblers and drinkers who had taken no notice of him before were now casting him covetous glances and laughing at some secret joke between them. Something was going on that concerned him that he did not know about and it seemed to stem from the whispering giant who had just entered. Even Gates was giving him an evil smile. He found out the reason a few minutes later when the big man, after slugging down the first drink, hefted the bottle and glass and turned in his direction. The negro going through what was obviously a routine, scuttled in a bent, cowed way towards him, hunkering down, chains clanking, against the wall near Matt.

The floor shook as Whispering Jake headed towards Matt and slammed the bottle and glass down on the table.

'You're sitting in my seat, mister,' Jake whispered, glaring down at him, and a silence fell through the room. Somehow word had even reached those engaged in more earthy pursuits in the upstairs rooms and they now stood in the doorways waiting and watching. Matt saw no reason to let the situation grow.

'Plumb sorry, mister. I'm new around here,' Matt said. 'You can have your seat back.' He went to rise, but with a nasty grin Jake used his thick thighs to push the table forward, pinning Matt against the wall, arms trapped beneath. Matt felt the edge of the table bite painfully into his ribs as Jake put more weight behind it and repeated his former statement.

'You're sitting in my seat, mister.'

Matt could feel the negro's eyes on him, pitying; and the anger he was trying to suppress rose.

'You shouldn't have sat in Jake's chair, mister, that was a sure, fool thing to do,' someone called and a general snigger ran around the room.

Jake leaned forward, hands on the table-top, thighs still grinding the edge of the table into Matt's ribs.

'I think I'll break your ribs,' he hissed, foul breath hissing over Matt's face.

Matt's eyes were bleak, grey chips as he stared back into the big, fleshy face.

'I think I'll blow your balls off, fat man,' Matt grated back and from beneath the table came the ominous clicking of a gun being cocked. Matt had drawn the weapon as Jake had approached.

Jake stiffened in the half-bent pose as a painful silence filled the room. 'And if you think a good shove of the table might save you, then you're dead.'

The two eyed each other and slowly Jake straightened. There was a heavy sweat on his face.

'Ain't no cause to get trigger-happy, fella,' he whispered, moving back half a step. His huge body was tense, eyes never leaving Matt.

Matt pushed the table forward with his free hand and brought the gun into view. Casually he reached for the bottle that Jake had slammed onto the table earlier and poured himself a drink.

'Why's the boy in chains?' Matt asked.

'Nigras should be in chains,' Jake whispered back, eyes flashing.

Matt sipped the drink, eyes on Jake.

'The key!' Matt's voice whiplashed out.

'Ain't got no key,' Jake hissed truculently.

Matt digested that piece of news, then, without warning, kicked the table aside, the bottle and remaining glass smashing on the floor. At the same time he angled the gun down and fired. The sound of the shot crashed about the room and a hole appeared in the boards less than an inch from Jake's left foot. Matt's eyes were wintry.

'I don't like to waste bullets. The next one will be in your fat gut. The key, or you'll be taken out of here horizontal.'

Jake looked into Matt's eyes, saw something he didn't like and fumbled in his pockets until he came up with a key. This he tossed on the floor near Matt's feet.

'I ain't fergettin' you, fella,' he hissed malevolently. 'You're already dead.'

'Boy, get the key and shuck those irons and then get the hell out of here. You're free.' He ignored Jake's threat and addressed himself to the negro, eyes never leaving Jake.

The negro looked up at Matt's profile dazedly. He could not believe his ears and it took a few seconds to sink in. When it did he clawed the key up and minutes later stood free of the chains.

'How long you been in those chains, boy?' Matt asked.

'Five years, boss,' he answered faintly and Matt's eyes grew colder as he looked at Jake.

'Get your boots off.'

'Look, fella . . . ' Jake began. The Schofield-Smith and Wesson exploded in Matt's hand. Jake gave a hoarse scream and clutched at his right ear, blood rolling down his neck. The lobe had been shot away.

'Get your boots off,' Matt said again. This time Jake did not argue. He quickly pulled his boots off and stood on dirty, bare feet holding a grubby bandanna to his damaged ear. 'Put the boots on, boy. They might be a trifle big, but they're better'n nothing.'

Grinning broadly now, the negro pulled the boots on.

'You'll never get away from here alive,' Jake promised.

'I figure you owe the boy some backpay. Give generously, fat man or I'll get the other ear.' Jake handed over his money and stared at Matt with sullen, hate-filled eyes.

'You've gone too far, fella.'

'And I've got a ways to go yet. Get, boy. Get offa this mountain. You're free now.'

'Mister. Ah . . . '

'Just get out, boy,' Matt said, not unkindly.

With a last grateful look at Matt and a glower at Jake, the negro darted through the batwings into the night.

'Less'n you kill me now, fella, you're gonna spend the rest of your life looking over your shoulder,' Jake smouldered in hissing rage.

Matt smiled bleakly as he downed the glass and hooked a foot under the chains and kicked them towards Jake.

'Put 'em on, fat man,' he said quietly, the command bringing gasps to some of the onlookers. Jake backed away.

'You'll have to kill me first,' he said.

'I ain't fussed,' Matt replied and thumbed the hammer back.

Fear leapt into Jake's eyes. He was always willing to take on a bluff, but the man's eyes said he wasn't bluffing. Tight-lipped, he put the irons about his ankles and turned the key in each one. Then duplicated the move with the wrist irons. His face was red from the effort of bending and shame for the way he was being made to crawl before the others.

'Fella — '

'The key.' Matt held out a hand, but Jake threw it at his feet.

'You're dead!' Jake hissed flatly.

'You will be if'n you're still here in five seconds,' Matt replied.

Jake stared at him murderously then clanked to the batwings. He paused for a final glare at Matt.

'I'm gonna enjoy your death, fella,' he promised and went out into the night.

Matt looked around the still silent room.

'If any of you have a notion to take on the fat man's battle I'm ready to oblige.' The challenge went unanswered and, with the drama over, the bar returned to normal.

Matt was shaking inside. He had not meant to make such an extrovert showing, but he had been forced into it. He returned the gun to its holster after reloading and hauled the table back onto its legs.

Carrying a bottle of whiskey and two glasses, Josiah Gates made his way across to Matt.

'The name's Gates, Josiah Gates, I own this place. Mind if I sit?'

'You own it, you sit,' Matt replied stiffly. He had seen two of Gate's men move quietly into position, one lounging against the wall to his left and the other dropping into a seat to his right.

'Figured you could use a drink, on the house, of course.' Gates smiled at his own generosity.

'And I figure that if your two boys try anything, Gates, you'll be the first to go.'

Gates face blanched.

'You don't miss much do you?' He forced a laugh as he filled two glasses.

'It's how I stay alive. Get rid of them before I start to get nervous.'

Gates waved the two away.

'You ain't too friendly are you, stranger?'

'Ain't got no cause to be and that's the way I like it.'

'Jake ain't gonna take too kindly to you. He makes a bad enemy.'

'I make an even worse one.'

'Do I know you from anywhere, Mr . . . Mr . . . ?'

'I appreciate the drink, Mr Gates, but not the conversation,' Matt said pointedly.

'Suit yourself, friend,' Gates replied stiffly. 'But if'n I was you I wouldn't hang around here too long. Whispering Jake's got powerful friends who might not take too kindly to what you done to him.'

'Is that a fact?' Matt sounded bored.

'Maybe you never heard of the Dukes,' Gates sneered. 'But young Billy ain't gonna be too happy that you let the darkie go. In case you didn't notice, that boy had a few toes missing. Billy Duke shot 'em off. He sure liked to see that darkie dance. Trouble was he was apt to shoot a toe off during the proceedings.' Gates giggled. 'We was all wondering what he was gonna shoot off when all the darkie's toes were gone.' Gates giggled again.

Matt remained unsmiling.

'That sense of humour's gonna get you killed one

day,' he said.

Gates stopped laughing.

'You won't be around to see it, mister. Billy's mighty slick with a gun and now you've spoiled his fun.'

'Live around here do they, these Dukes?' Matt asked casually.

'Maybe,' Gates said cautiously. 'They come in occasionall . . . .' He broke off as someone came through the batwings and his face blanched. 'You're dead, mister,' he said throatily, grabbing the bottle and coming to his feet. 'Billy Duke's just come in.' He scuttled back to his seat at the end of the bar.

Another figure followed close behind Billy, chains clanking, and for the second time in an evening the room went quiet.

Neither Billy or Jake looked in Matt's direction as they stomped to the bar. At the sight of Billy's slim shoulders and golden hair tumbling from beneath the dark hat, Matt's heart quickened.

'Evening, Billy,' Josiah Gates sang out. 'Drink on the house for Billy.'

'Better make that a bottle, Gates. I aim to do some killing and that sure is thirsty work.'

Matt could see Billy's face in the mirror behind the bar and saw that the reflected image was staring at him.

The bottle and glasses came quickly. Billy filled two glasses to the brim as the tension in the room mounted. The doors above opened, as girls and clients emerged silently.

Billy drained his glass in a single gulp and turned,

leaning casually back, elbows on the bar, while his blue eyes fastened onto Matt's downcast head.

'Heared you set the nigger free and put the irons on Jake.' His blue eyes appraised the seated man.

Matt lifted his head and for a flash, as their eyes locked, Billy's brows knitted in recognition, but it was gone in an instant.

'Ain't nothing wrong with your ears or eyes,' Matt acknowledged and came slowly to his feet, side-stepping away from the table. Matt remembered the face of Billy Duke, laughing when his brother Rafe had put a bullet in Ben. Laughing when Jack had pushed the cactus thorns into the soles of his feet. Laughing and joking all the way. A tremor of rage shook Matt as white-hot anger seared through his brain.

'Can you dance, mister?' Billy was smiling now and Jake gave his peculiar, hissing laugh that was taken up by others in the room.

'Bet he's a real sweet mover,' someone called.

'Set him a-dancing, Billy,' a second voice urged.

'Hear you're fancy with a gun, mister.'

'Hear you're fancy with your mouth,' Matt replied and the laughter in the room faded to silence.

The smile disappeared from Billy's face. He was used to men grovelling, begging for mercy. This was something new and he didn't like it. The man showed no fear.

'Do you want to die that bad, mister?' he asked softly and came away from the bar, arms loose at his sides, right hand hovering near the butt of his .45.

'I'm not dead yet,' Matt pointed out.

'Just who are you, mister?' Billy asked as fear made its presence known in his mind and he pushed it aside. 'Need a name for the headstone.' Faces on the edge of Billy's vision smiled, bolstering the man's flagging confidence.

A bleak smile settled on Matt's bearded features.

'Your worst nightmare, Billy. The man that's gonna kill you,' he replied quietly.

Billy went for his gun in an expert, fluid movement. It was a lightning move that brought gasps from the onlookers. The .45 was levelling at Matt's chest when a bullet from Matt's Schofield-Smith and Wesson punched a hole in Billy's midriff and threw him back against the edge of the bar.

A woman screamed.

Billy grabbed at the blossom of red that spread across his shirt-front, a look of disbelief in his blue eyes. He lifted his gun weakly, and a second bullet took him between the eyes and opened the back of his head in a spray of red and grey that splattered the mirror behind the bar in a gory mist. The gun in Billy's hand exploded as his finger convulsed on the trigger in a death spasm, the bullet burying itself in the boards of the floor. Billy was dead before his body slid down the front of the bar and toppled sideways.

Everyone seemed frozen to the spot as Matt returned the gun to its holster and stared, expressionless, at the still body.

Josiah Gates clung to the edge of the bar, his eyes wide with disbelief at the impossible sight he had just witnessed.

'You've just killed Billy Duke,' he gasped weakly, sweat standing out on his face. 'When Pappy finds out what you done, mister, you ain't gonna find a place that will hide you.'

'You got it wrong, Gates. I won't be through until every one of those Dukes is dead. Tell him I'll be looking for him and the boys.'

Gates studied the set, hard-eyed face.

'What name shall I tell him?'

'Death!' Matt replied bleakly. He turned abruptly and went out into the night and let the cool, pine-scented air fill his lungs.

SEVEN

A cool, white mist drifted from the shallow, tumbling stream that sang and gurgled over glistening pebbles and around dry-topped rocks. It ran like liquid silver along the bottom of the pine-banked gully. Already the morning sun was sending pale fingers of light shafting through the trees in ghostly beams.

Matt had finished a frugal breakfast of beans and jerky after spending a night bedded down in the gully and he now tipped the dregs from his coffee-cup onto the ground. He kicked dry, dusty earth over the small fire and hunkered down by the stream to scour off his cup and plate. It was his intention now to draw the Dukes to him. Killing Billy would bring them out. He wouldn't have to go looking for them, they would be looking for him and he would be waiting. He intended to take up a position overlooking Mountain Bend and wait. Sooner or later the Dukes would come in and he expected sooner, once the news of Billy's death reached them. A wan smile touched his face. He had stirred up a hornets' nest. He only hoped he could handle the resultant explosion.

The bay whickered and tossed its head. Matt arose and peered about, before moving across to the horse and rubbing a hand over its muzzle.

'Easy, boy. Nothing to be scared of,' he breathed and the bay pushed its muzzle against his hand. Soothing words to the horse, but Matt found himself listening intently, trying to pick out and identify individual sounds above the chatter and gurgle of the water. Stealthy sounds. Small, furtive scurryings in the mist-enveloped undergrowth that he put down to animal rather than man.

Matt had just completed strapping his bed-roll in place on the saddle, a low, tuneless whistle blowing from his lips, when he turned and found himself staring into the fat, grinning face of Whispering Jake. How the man had got in so close without being heard was a mystery to Matt, but a mystery he had no time to dwell on. A section of tree branch as thick as his leg and longer was swinging in a bone-breaking arc towards him.

It caught him just under the ribs, exploding the breath from his body and sending him crashing back against the bay. The big horse whinneyed in alarm and danced sideways, shod hooves beating out a tattoo of panic on the stony ground. He bounced off the bay's flanks, clutching at his ribs in agony. He heard Jake's wheezing laugh and the branch came down across his shoulders and smashed him face down into the earth as he tried to pull his gun. The pain that clawed through his shoulders had a paralyzing effect that numbed his arms. His head was roaring as he rolled, groaning, on to his back to stare up through blurred eyes at the massive figure looming over him. The chains were gone. Jake stopped and pulled the gun from Matt's holster, tossing it casually aside.

'Don' need that shit to take you, drifter,' he whispered. 'You made a fool of Jake. Set his nigra free and killed Billy. I ain't gonna kill yer, fella. I'm gonna leave that to Pappy. Word's gone out to him and he's gonna feel real mean.' Jake lifted a booted foot and stamped down on Matt's genitals. Matt screamed hoarsely as knife-like shards of pain ripped up through his groin and stabbed at his stomach, making him vomit his breakfast over the ground. He rolled on to his side, hands between his legs, knees drawn up. 'Gonna have me some fun first,' Jake promised, gleefully.

Jake pounded him a few more times with the branch before tossing it aside and hauling the near-unconscious Matt to his feet. Matt hung in the huge man's hands like a limp rag-doll, the toes of his boots barely touching the ground. His head spun and pain seemed to flare from every part of his body.

'Didn't think you could be found eh, Mr Fast Gun?' Jake's foul breath washed over Matt's face. 'Didn't reckon on ol' Jake creeping up on you as light as a feather.' Jake vented his wheezing chuckle, then his face grew serious. 'Mebbe I'll kill you anyway and save Pappy the job.' As though he had no more weight than a child, Jake tossed the limp form of Matt from him.

Matt saw a kaleidoscope of trees, earth and sky

before bouncing on the hard-packed, stony ground that edged the stream. Elbows, head and buttocks felt the savage edge of rock and stone as the impetus rolled him into the ice-cold water and he lay face down. The shock of the cold water helped revive him. He reared up on hands and knees, gasping and spluttering. Blood ran from a gash on his forehead, mingled with the water and covered his face with a patchy red mask.

He heard the crunch of boots on stone, then splashing as Jake came towards him. Matt could see him approaching from the corner of one eye. His hands closed around a smooth, brown, fist-sized pebble and he waited for Jake to come within reach. Jake was smiling as he reached the kneeling man, but the smile left his face as Matt's fists, wrapped about the pebble, swung up into his bulging gut.

Jake's eyes popped and air whooshed from his lips. Matt came to his feet and swung his hands at Jake's chin. The blow rocked the man, snapped his head to one side, but there was a grin on his fat face as he looked back at Matt.

'Gotta do better'n that, Fancy Gun,' he hissed and lashed out with a tremendous back-hander. It caught Matt on the side of the chin and he spun like a top until a rock tangled his feet and he splashed face down again into the shallow, swirling water. As he lifted his face clear, Jake placed a foot on the back of Matt's neck and pushed his head back under, holding it there.

Matt thrashed about in wild panic, unable to free himself. Water filled his nostrils and trickled down the back of his throat. Jake ground his foot down hard, pushing Matt's face deeper into the gravel that lined the stream bed, rolling it from side to side.

Pain tore Matt's lips open and water rushed in in a never-ending torrent to flood down his throat into his lungs, choking and smothering. A roaring filled his ears and his struggles grew weaker. His arms and legs felt like lead and a peculiar lightness filled his head and he no longer fought the weight holding him down. The weight was suddenly removed and his face was hauled clear of the water. He coughed and retched water from his lungs.

'We don' want you a-dying too quick.' Jake's voice seemed to come from the far end of a long tunnel. Hauling Matt by the back of his collar, Jake dragged him from the water and dumped him on the ground.

Matt lay there, clawing at the earth as convulsions shook his body. Jake used a foot to flip him over on to his back.

'Ain't right you should have made ol' Jake look a fool,' he whispered. 'No sirree.' Jake looked hard at Matt before pulling a broad-bladed hunting knife from a sheath. 'Learned how to scalp a man once. Take off all the skin and hair right down to the bone.' His small eyes blazed and a look of delight filled his face.

Matt stared up at the grinning face, tasting the metallic tang of blood in his mouth from lips that were mashed and puffy. He gathered all his remaining strength into one last effort. Lifting both feet and pulling his knees back to his chest, he kicked out.

The blow took Jake by surprise and this time had

the desired effect. Caught just above the belt buckle the big man took a half-step back then sat heavily on his rump. Ignoring the pain, Matt scrambled to his feet. His only chance was to get to a gun. He was not sure where the pistol had been tossed, so his only hope was the rifle on the bay. For all the layers of fat that covered Jake's body like layers of clay, the man was immensely strong. In hand-to-hand fighting Matt had little chance. His legs felt like rubber and he weaved like a drunken man as he fought to keep his balance.

The effort caused his head to spin and vision blur and with a cry of anguish his legs gave way beneath him and he sprawled on the ground, coughing blood from his damaged lips that filled his mouth. Slowly, using his hands, he dragged himself forward, heart hammering fit to bust in his chest. Ahead the mist appeared to be thickening, making the bay a dark shadow within it.

Jake was back to his feet and seeing that Matt was not going to get very far, followed him in a leisurely fashion, enjoying the man's futile efforts.

'Ain't nowhere to go, Mr Fast Gun,' Jake wheezed.

Matt came to a halt and turned himself over, levering himself up on elbows to regard his fat tormentor.

'You won't kill me, Jake,' Matt shot back thickly. 'Pappy Duke would slit your throat for spoiling his pleasure.'

Jake scowled down at Matt, the smile fading. His face became screwed with thought then smoothed beneath a smile.

'Guess I'll jus' have to work on you a little and leave enough of you alive for Pappy to finish off.' He bobbed his head to indicate he liked the idea and ran a thick thumb along the edge of the knife.

The rifle shot came as a complete surprise to both men. Within the confines of the gully it deafened Matt. Jake staggered as though he had received a punch in the stomach and stared down with disbelief as the dirty, grey shirt he wore turned red just above the belt buckle. He slapped a fat hand over the spreading redness and stared beyond Matt. Matt craned his head around. The rising sun was rapidly burning the mist away, reducing it to thick, drifting clouds at ground level. At first he saw nothing then from the mist stepped the figure of the negro slave that Matt had freed the night before and in his hands he gripped Matt's Winchester.

'Yer don' keep me in chains for five years, fat man. Beating on muh body until I was near dead. I knowed that one day I'd get free and the first thing I promised myself to do was to kill you.' He levered another shell into the breech of the rifle as he spoke.

White-faced, sweat standing out in beads, Jake raised a hand, and the rifle roared again, fired from hip-level as the negro stepped closer. The bullet slammed Jake high in the chest to the right and the huge man sank to his knees, still gripping his stomach, the knife dropped earlier. His piggy eyes pleaded with the negro, looking for mercy in the black face and finding none. He staggered to his feet as blood exploded through his teeth and ran down his chin. The rifle spoke again and the right-hand side of Jake's face exploded in a shower of bone and blood as the skull shattered under the impact of the bullet.

Jake went down. His gross body convulsed twice, heels scraping ruts in the earth, then lay still.

The negro's shoulders slumped, as though Jake's death had sucked something from him. He turned away, almost wearily, from the still form and approached Matt, eyes growing at Matt's battered appearance. He hunkered down at Matt's side, concern on his dark face.

'You all right, boss?'

'Better than he is.' The words came thick and slurred from Matt's cut and swollen lips. One eye was almost closed and blood covered his face in a mesh of red. 'What the hell are you doing still here? I figured you'd be long gone by now.'

'Had some unfinished business, boss. 'Sides, ain't no place left to go. Black boy with money in his pockets and the marks of irons on his wrists and legs ain't gonna get far in a white town.'

'The name's Matt, not boss. How do they call you, boy?'

'Jethro if I 'member right. Ain't heard it for a long time.'

'Well help me up, Jethro, if'n you'd be so kind.'

Muscles and joints screamed a protest as Jethro helped him to his feet. Matt bit back the cries that rose to his lips. It seemed to him that everything that could hurt did hurt.

'Whispering Jake sure beat up on you,

bo . . . Matt,' Jethro said.

'You don't have to tell me. Set me on yonder rock while I try to figure out if'n I'm alive or dead.' Once he was seated, Matt eyed Jethro. 'I thank you, Jethro. If you hadn't happened along Jake and I would have changed places by now. How did you happen to be here?'

'Like I said. Ain't no place for a black boy out there. Figured I'd stay on the mountain, but first I had to take care of Jake. I hung around town. I see'd you leave, but Jake stayed the night and didn't leave till sun-up. I started following him and got interested when he didn't head for home. Figured he musta picked up your trail, then I lost him in the mist. Took a time afore I came upon his horse at the head of the gully and came on down.'

'Well I'm mighty glad you did.' Matt climbed gingerly to his feet. The pains had reduced to dull aches and his head had cleared. He peeled off his coat and shirt, wincing as bruised muscles protested. He made his way down to the stream and stepped out of his wet breeches and under-drawers and found a sink-hole in the water to sit in and let the icy water numb his bruised and battered flesh. Jethro was sitting on the rock when Matt returned, carrying his damp clothes. He spread them out on another slab that a ray of sunlight was warming before fetching a square of towel from his saddlebag to dry himself.

Jethro had found Matt's handgun and after Matt had pulled on a set of fresh clothes, handed it to him.

'Why is you still here, Matt?' It was the first words that had passed between the two for quite a while. 'I done heard men talking last night that you kilt Billy Duke. The Dukes are mean folk and they'll be a-looking for you.'

Matt gave a smile that pained his lips and he paused as he buttoned his brown shirt.

'Like you, Jethro. I got some unfinished business.'

'With the Dukes?' Jethro fairly yelled, eyes rolling as Matt fastened the last button and tucked the shirt-tails into his pants.

'I'm obliged you hung around, boy, but from now on it's not gonna be too healthy to be seen with me.'

'Ain't too healthy being a black boy,' Jethro pointed out, slipping from the rock and moving to the head of the bay to gently stroke the velvety muzzle. 'Figure we might be stuck with each other for a while.'

'Where you from, Jethro?'

'Georgia, 'riginally. A whole bunch of black families lit out to Texas aiming to buy a little land to homestead.'

'What happened?'

''Paches,' Jethro spat. 'They killed everyone 'cept me. I managed to make it to the mountains and that's where I met up with Jake.'

'Hell, I'm sorry, boy. Didn't mean to spark memories,' Matt said.

'It was a time ago,' Jethro shrugged. 'I done muh grieving. So you see I ain't got no place to go now.' He handed back the rifle. 'What you gonna do now?'

'Wait for the Dukes to come looking for me and take it from there.'

'Ain't much of a plan.'

'Ain't much of anything, but it's the best I got.'

'Could mebbe help you with a better one,' Jethro said, after a thoughtful silence.

Matt's brows furrowed as he looked at Jethro.

'How come?'

'I know where the Dukes hideout is.'

Jethro's freedom after five years of forced slavery in the hands of Whispering Jake was short-lived. He died three hours later.

Conversation between the two had been sparse after leaving the gully, but during the earlier part of the journey Matt learned that Jake had taken Jethro to the Dukes' place on a number of occasions. At these times they had drunk themselves into a stupor and then made Jethro dance and caper in his chains using his feet as target practice. Matt could only admire the man for the courage and strength of mind that had been needed to survive those five, terrible years.

With Jethro in the lead the two followed faint, narrow trails through the trees. Trails that climbed and dipped. Sometimes they ran beside walls of grey rock that rose sheer to the sky above. Other times the green gloom of dense forest swallowed them. The sun was high in the sky by the time Jethro came to a halt in a small clearing and it was time to walk the last bit.

The terrain was a jumble of massive rocks, pine and brush and was scattered with stunted, twisted scrub-oak. Massive walls of rock broke above the treetops. The cabin was set in a clearing and was

flanked on either side by stands of pine. On two sides
the towering cliffs rose skyward. The third side was a
steep slope of rock and pine where the two were now
crouched behind a scrub thicket. The fourth side
opened up to reveal the tops of pines rising from the
lower slopes that gave way to rolling hills. The
horizon was a slash of gold that merged with a purple
smudge into the blue of the sky. In that direction lay
the desert flats. Though Matt didn't know it, this was
the Dukes' second hideout.

There were five horses hitched outside the cabin.

'Looks like the pony express from Mountain Bend
has arrived already,' Matt whispered to Jethro.

Jethro bobbed his head in agreement and that was
when the rifle slug took him in the back, shattering
his spine and leaving him dead.

EIGHT

Matt rolled to the left as Jethro's face slammed into the dust, blood jetting from his lips. A second bullet buzzed like an angry hornet into the thicket where his head had been only seconds before.

'I got him spotted, Mr Gates,' a triumphant voice bawled from the trees back of Matt. 'Shot the lousy nigra dead.'

In the cabin Josiah Gates jumped at the sound of the shot then relaxed when he heard the voice. As Rafe and Jack jumped up from the table where they all sat, Gates smiled confidently at the sour-faced old man at the end.

'Like I said, Pappy. The *hombre* that killed Billy ain't gonna get away.' It stunk in the cabin. A mixture of unwashed bodies, urine and vomit. The Dukes were animals and lived like animals.

'I want him, Gates,' Pappy said low and hard, thin hands balling into fists on the soiled table-top.

'He's yours, Pappy,' Gates offered expansively, trying not to wrinkle his nose at the smell.

'See anythin'?' Pappy snapped at Rafe and Jack who had positioned themselves either side of the grimy window.

'Not a blamed thing,' Rafe replied.

'He'd better not get away, Gates,' Pappy shot warningly at Gates. The news that Billy was dead had hit Pappy hard. 'How many men you got out there?'

'Six. Six good boys, Pappy.'

Pappy came to his feet scowling at Gates, making the man shake inside and barged Jake aside at the window.

'Hey, out there,' Pappy shouted. 'Keep the son-of-a-bitch alive. I want him.'

It was at that moment that the Gates man doing the crowing showed a little too much of himself. Matt snapped a shot at him with his pistol. It took the man in the throat just above the adam's apple and threw him backwards in a cascade of red.

'Morgan's dead, Mr Gates.' A new voice came from up the slope to Matt's right, probably from the stand of pine and brush. The area he now fought in was virtually on the side of a hill. It was an area that couldn't make up its mind whether to be forest or mountain so did a bad job of both. Rocks and boulders littered the green slope and tangled with stands of stunted scrub-oak and thickets of thorn and brush. They dotted the slope in patches leaving large open areas. To gain the denser, forested areas meant either going up or across and both areas appeared to be covered.

Matt groaned to himself. With Gates in the cabin spilling everything to the Dukes, he had left his bully-boys posted about and now Matt was surrounded. One had got careless and paid the full price, the others would show a little more caution. He had been far too complacent. Sure he had expected someone to hightail it to the Dukes place. He was not surprised to find it was Gates. But where Gates had been astute enough to position men in hiding against the possibility of Matt turning up, Matt had not anticipated any such action being taken. Gates had no way of knowing that Matt did not know where the Dukes hideout was, nor the fact that he would team up with Jethro who did. All he had done was take the simplest precautions against a surprise visit and Matt had walked straight into it. The result of which was that Jethro now lay dead and he had a good chance of following suit.

A bullet raised dust and rock splinters near his face as he risked a peep down the slope, and whining off into the sky. It had come from behind where he was crouched, up the slope. The aches and pains of his body forgotten, Matt dived between two rocks as a second bullet ricocheted into the sky with a thin scream.

'I got him pinned,' the hidden gunman yelled.

'Keep him alive,' Matt heard Pappy yell again and smiled thinly. The order gave him an edge that otherwise he would not have had. He needed to bring the hidden man out from above, for in that direction lay his possible way out. It was time for a little play-acting. He purposely showed himself to the hidden man and almost felt the breeze of the bullet pass by. He gave a loud, theatrical cry, grabbed at his body and fell, lying still on his front, head turned to give him a view up the slope, pistol still clasped in an outflung hand. He had fallen in such a way as to be shielded from below by the rocks.

'He's down,' the hidden man called and Matt detected an anxious note in the voice. Tough as the men were, they were afraid of the Dukes.

'If'n you've done killed him, you'll stand in his place,' Pappy threatened, tumbling from the cabin with the others hot on his heels.

Matt was gambling on the man coming to investigate to see if he was dead or merely winged. The seconds dragged into minutes and Matt remained still. He could hear voices in the direction the cabin lay and knew that Pappy and the boys were on the way up.

He was beginning to feel that he had lost his gamble when there was movement from above and a man stepped from the cover of a stand of pines fronted by a thicket of scrub. He was about a hundred yards uphill. Matt's heart thumped against the earth as he willed him to come closer, but the man seemed content to stand and look.

Matt heard Pappy shout something and the voice seemed awfully close. He knew he could not risk waiting much longer. The man seemed to make up his mind and began moving down the slope towards him, moving quickly. Matt waited until the distance had been halved and the man was out in the open before scrambling to his knees and aiming the pistol. The man had enough impetus to keep coming down and not move to the side. Matt fired off two bullets. Both hit the man and his co-ordinated run became a tumbling mass of arms and legs.

Two other figures were approaching the rocks from the trees across the slope, one from below the other. Matt fired at the one advancing across the slope and felt a savage satisfaction as the man folded in on himself and fell. The one advancing up the slope dived for cover. Matt hauled himself up and crouching charged up the slope.

'What's happening?' Pappy yelled. They had all dived for cover at the first shot.

'The bastard was lying doggo,' a voice called back. 'Cleat's dead and Quinlan.'

Matt zigzagged up the slope keeping as much of the sparse cover he could between himself and the other gunmen. It was punishing on the legs. Bullets buzzed angrily at his heels, but finally he reached the stand of trees and dived behind the brush thicket, dragging air into his gasping lungs. There were enough gaps in the scrub to see through without being seen. He loosed off the rest of his bullets at the Dukes, sending them scattering for cover. Josiah Gates was not so lucky. A bullet caught him in the mouth, destroying most of his jaw before it punched its way out through the back of his neck.

Matt quickly reloaded from his gunbelt. Gates had at least six men on his pay-roll. Three were dead, one down the slope and that left two unaccounted for. Matt squinted through the brush, but for the moment everyone had gone to ground and a nervous silence settled over the slope.

The sound of a weapon being cocked from behind froze Matt.

'Well lookee what we done got ourselves here,' a gruff voice goaded. Matt spun around on his knees and looked up to find two rifles trained on him; he had found the other two men. They stood at the top of grassy bank behind him. Big, unsmiling men, eyes hard in their stubble-rimmed faces. 'Toss the piece,' Gruff voice snarled.

With a sinking heart, Matt let the weapon drop.

'Sure is a good thing we'uns hung back, Sam,' the second man brayed out in a nasal tone and let a smile haunt his thin features.

'Ain't that a pure fact, Chuck,' the first mused, then shouted, 'we done got him, Pappy, disarmed and ready for you. Stand up, boy and scratch sky and let 'em get a look at you.'

Tight-lipped, Matt came to his feet and moved clear of the thicket. Pappy, Rafe and Jack were on their feet and staring up the slope.

'You killed my boy, Matt Holder, now I'm gonna make you wish you were dead,' he shouted.

Behind Matt the two gunmen scrambled down the bank and Chuck retrieved Matt's gun and stuck it in his belt.

Matt was surprised at the use of his name by Pappy Duke. He had told no one his name in Mountain Bend, so it was a mystery how the old man knew it.

'You might of escaped the desert, boy, but you'll never get off this mountain alive, not with what we've got planned for you. Bring him down boys, I'm getting real impatient to start.'

The one called Sam had drifted alongside Matt's right-hand side, the rifle hanging loose in his right hand. Matt could see Chuck from the corner of his eye, behind and to the left. Both men had relaxed now. Matt had been disarmed, the danger was over.

During his stay in Yuma he had spent some time with a Chinaman and the man had taught him a peculiar method of fighting using the edge of the hand and straight fingers to hit with rather than a clenched fist. It also entailed using the feet. Once a group of five prisoners had decided to beat the Chinaman up. Though smaller than his attackers, the lightning moves the man had made with his feet and hands had amazed Matt. It amazed him even more when the five bigger men were stretched out on the ground. Charlie Fong had taught Matt the rudiments of a method of fighting called 'Kung Fu', now he hoped he hadn't forgotten how. Licking his lips, Matt tensed.

'You heard what the man said, boy. Move on down.' Sam half turned to Matt and was still smiling when the edge of Matt's right hand chopped savagely into his throat crushing the windpipe. As the man stumbled back, dropping the rifle and clutching at his throat, Matt spun on his left leg and leapt into the air lashing out with his right foot and catching Chuck high on the chest. The blow sent the man crashing down on his back, crying out in his surprise. He tried to bring the rifle into play, only to have it kicked from his hands. Matt hauled his pistol from the man's belt and crashed the barrel across the man's mouth, splitting his lips and breaking teeth.

Chuck howled his pain as blood squirted between fingers he put to his mouth. Bullets began to fly about Matt as those below realized what was happening.

'Don't let him get away,' Pappy raved. 'Don't let him get away.' He fairly danced his rage as Matt vanished from sight behind the brush thicket. 'After him!'

By the time the Dukes reached the trees, followed by the last of Gates's gunmen, Matt had vanished. Pausing only to grab the moaning Chuck's rifle, he scaled the bank and disappeared into the trees.

Pappy Duke stared about, wild-eyed.

'Where'd he go?' he demanded of the injured man. Chuck could not speak, but he indicated 'up'. 'You let him get away,' Pappy fumed and shot Chuck between the eyes. Then he turned the gun on the choking, gagging Sam. Finally he turned to face Carson, the last of Gates's men. Fear turned the gunman's face chalky.

'I didn't do nothing, Mr Duke,' he pleaded, backing away, eyes flitting from one grim face to the other.

Pappy regarded him coolly.

'I guess you didn't, boy,' he said softly and pumped two bullets into the man's chest. 'So you ain't no good to me.' He turned to the grinning Rafe and Jack. 'Let's go git him afore he realizes that he's run himself into a corner.'

Matt was already finding that out. A steep, thirty-foot climb brought him out of the trees and into the sunlight of a wide, rock platform set at the base of a sheer, towering rock wall. To his left the platform narrowed rapidly and ended in a fifty-foot drop. He ran to the right, feeling the heat of the sun bounce away from the wall and flood over him only to find, to his dismay, that the platform narrowed again and finally vanished altogether. The platform of rock was shapped like half a dish. He realised with a shock of frustration that the only way off the platform was the way he had come and the Dukes were already blocking that.

The cliff face was unscaleable and the only breach in its smooth surface was a cave set near the end to the right. It was his only means of cover and he ducked in. He barely made it as a fusillade of bullets followed his disappearing back. The Dukes had arrived. He had heard the earlier shots and guessed grimly that it was the Dukes clearing up the loose ends in their own bloody fashion.

As more bullets peppered the entrance, Matt retreated back into the darkness to crouch behind a slab of rock waiting, with rifle in hand, for anyone foolish enough to appear at the entrance.

'How we gonna get him out, pa?' Jack wanted to know, lank strands of black hair clawing at his fat, sweating face. His grubby blue shirt was dark with sweat.

'Can't stay in there forever,' Rafe pointed out. 'Ain't got food or water. Starve to death more'n likely.'

'We gotta wait that long?' Jack fairly howled. 'We gotta wait here forever, pa?' His heavy face creased in dismay at the prospect.

'Ain't got the time for that. Got things to do,' Pappy said. 'If'n that boy wants to stay in there, then we'd best oblige him.' He allowed himself a smile. 'Get on back to the cabin, Jack and bring back a couple o' those sticks of dynamite we's been keeping for a special occasion.'

Jack's dismay grew at the thought of returning to the cabin and then coming back again.

'Can't Rafe go, pa?'

'I asked you, boy. Now don't sass me none.'

'But why me, pa?' Jack persisted miserably.

'Cause you're fat and need to lose some o' that lard. Now git afore I take my belt to you.'

'That's the truth, pa. He sure do wobble a lot,' Rafe chortled, glorying in his brother's discomfort.

'It ain't right,' Jack muttered casting Rafe a wicked stare.

'Ain't right that Billy's dead, boy and the son-of-a-bitch that done it's still alive. Now git that dynamite. There ain't but one way in and out of that cave and we're gonna seal it up real tight. Mr Dead Man don't know it yet, but he's a-sitting in his own tomb.'

'Hey that's good, pa,' Rafe applauded, exposing his big, crooked teeth in a smile that reduced to a scowl at Jack still standing there. 'Ain't you gone yet, Jack?'

'I'm going,' Jack said sullenly. 'Ain't right a body should have to do so much climbing. Could get a busted heart.'

'You'll git a busted head if'n you don't shift yourself,' Pappy replied. 'And don't take too long about it.'

After the grumbling Jack had departed, the two moved closer to the cave entrance, pressing themselves back against the rock wall.

'Ain't no place to go, Holder, but out the same way you went in.'

'Seems that would be a fool thing to do,' Matt shouted back. 'Of course you can always come in and get me.'

'Seems that would be a fool thing to do as well,' Pappy jeered back. 'We can wait, boy. Got all the time in the world. Got food, got water. Sure as hell can wait. How about you?'

'I'll make out.' Matt was grimly aware of how dry his throat was.

'They call the cave, "Devil's Hole" on accounts it leads straight to hell.' Pappy chuckled. 'Back o' the cave, if'n you ain't see'd it already, is a tunnel. Don't go but a short way's afore it drops straight down to hell. Plumb goes all the way down through this mountain. So don't figure on taking a long walk.' Pappy chuckled again.

Matt peered around as Pappy spoke and now that his eyes had got used to the darkness at the back of the cave he could make out the blacker opening of the tunnel, behind and a few yards to the right of where he crouched.

'I'll remember that,' he called back.

'You do that, Holder, cause you ain't ever coming outta that hell-hole. Should'a killed you in the desert.'

'How come you know my name?' Matt was curious.

'Coupla friends of your'n came visiting a while back. Wanted us to kill you for $500. Seems you smoked their tails in Larkinsville. Coupla nice young fellas. Seemed a right shame to kill 'em.' Pappy sounded almost regretful.

The Larkins boys, Matt thought bitterly. Well they'd paid the ultimate price.

'I'm sure you felt right sorry,' Matt said sarcastically.

'I allus do,' Pappy replied. 'I 'member one time . . . ' For the next thirty minutes Pappy recounted tales of the murderous deeds he and his hideous family had committed until Matt felt physically sick. It was only on the return of Jack, fat face shining with sweat, that the tirade stopped. Pappy took the two sticks of dynamite, both primed with lengths of fuse, stuffed one in his pocket and searched for a match. 'The jawing's over now, Holder. Time for you to die and us to travel.' He scowled as he spoke, hand diving from pocket to pocket until he found a match and the smile returned. 'Got some holy business at Desert Rock.'

A cold feeling washed over Matt.

'What do you mean?'

'Seems that a bunch of sisters done saved your life. It figures that if'n they had left you Billy would still be alive. They killed Billy, so they gotta be taught a lesson.' He struck the match on the rock wall and held it to the fuse until the cordite-impregnated cord began to spark and splutter, chewing its way towards the stick.

'You leave them alone,' Matt shouted hoarsely, coming to his feet.

'Can't do that, Holder. They gotta learn it ain't

safe to meddle in what don't concern them. 'Sides, Rafe here ain't never funned with a holy lady. 'Bout time he got some religion.' The fuse had reached the halfway point and both Rafe and Jack were edging away from Pappy.

'I killed Billy, not them!' Matt shouted.

'They gotta be taught,' Pappy said, moving to get an angled view of the cave mouth. He tossed the dynamite stick in. 'It's dying time, Holder,' he crowed and darted away from the entrance.

Matt was already moving forward, intending to rush from the cave and take his chances, when the dynamite hit the floor and rolled to the side just inside the entrance. He stopped in mid-stride, then turned and ran back, diving behind the rock slab that earlier he had been crouching behind. As he hit the floor, a deafening explosion rocked the cave and pounded at his eardrums.

Fragments and chunks of rock rolled in a blanket of dust, smoke enveloped him, and with a rumbling crack the roof of the cave collapsed and the entrance vanished.

NINE

Matt covered his head as pieces of rock rained down, slamming against his body and legs. A choking, stinging dust pricked his eyes and filled his flaring nostrils as it billowed over him. The roar of the explosion echoed around him, punishing his eardrums before it found release in the tunnel and fled, booming and crashing into the bowels of the mountain. Matt lay still for some minutes after the echoes had died away, his ears singing.

He moved cautiously, pieces of rock tumbling from his body as he twisted himself into a sitting position. There was a moment of panic when he realized his eyes were open, but he saw nothing but a velvety blackness. He fought the panic back as he searched for a match. He went through every pocket and came up with five. He struck one on the stone floor, screwing his eyes up against the initial flare.

Dust drifted through the flaming head of the match. Holding it aloft Matt saw a jumble of rock forming a wall just a few feet away. The entrance was a good ten or more feet beyond that. Matt winced and dropped the match as the flame licked at his fingers. In the ensuing darkness he acknowledged that Pappy had done a good job. No cracks of light broke through the wall; it was solid.

Matt remained there sitting back on his heels for several minutes letting his mind absorb the terrible truth: that he was entombed in the mountain. But uppermost in his mind was the revenge sworn by Pappy Duke against the Sisters of Mercy. Matt thought of the gentle, kind women, married to God and content to eke out a spartan existence on the edge of a wilderness in their devotion to Him. The thought of them in the hands of Rafe and Jack made him feel sick, but spurred him into action. There had to be another way out, if only he could find it. Not wishing to waste his precious matches he crawled forward on hands and knees to where he remembered the tunnel lay. Searching with his hands he found it and crawled in.

He remembered Pappy's words about the tunnel dropping right through the mountain and probed the rocky floor ahead with his hands before proceeding.

He collided with the rock fall that blocked the tunnel and ran his hands over the rough angles the surface presented. As his hands flickered over it, disturbing small stones that fell with a dry clatter, he rose on creaking knees. His knees were still bent when his head touched the roof. He pulled a second match and stroked it against rock, this time shielding his eyes with a splay-fingered hand. The initial flare revealed a chamber four feet high by three feet wide. He let the match burn down as he examined the fall. It looked as solid as the other. As the match went out he tossed it aside and sat wearily down, back to the wall. He was well and truly trapped.

How long he sat there listening to his own shallow breathing, he had no idea. It was the itch of sweat trickling down his face that jerked him back to reality. It had grown hot and stuffy. He ran a hand over his damp face, swallowing on a desert-dry throat. It was then he saw a paleness at the bottom far corner of the fall. He blinked, held out a trembling hand and saw his fingers, dark against the grey glow. With a quickening heart he scrambled forward and laid his head on the ground. He could see light and feel cooler air fanning his face.

He probed the area with a shaking hand and found loose rock. Quickly he began to pull the rock fragments clear, widening the gap. He worked feverishly for ten minutes until he had cleared a wedge-shaped gap and the light came through stronger. He peered through, but the tunnel curved to the right and he could see nothing of the source of the light. He looked to see if he could widen the gap further, but in the increased light he saw that a large slab had fallen from the roof to lean at an angle against the wall. The gap was as wide as it was ever going to be. Eight or nine inches at the most and narrowing down to nothing. It had looked large at first, but with the idea of squeezing through it, it seemed to visibly shrink. Not liking the idea at all, Matt stripped off his coat and unbuckled his gunbelt, these he pushed through first.

He tried squeezing through on his front, arms going first, but his shoulders jammed. He tried on his back, arms over his head, but his chest snagged. The only way left was on his back, arms at his sides, using feet to propel him through. The idea scared him. If he should get stuck with his arms pinned at his sides . . .

He put the idea from his mind as he began to wriggle through the narrow gap and the hard rock closed about him like a stone vice. He had to turn his head to one side as the rock above scraped his nose. Sweat pumped from his body as he pushed with his feet forcing himself deeper into the gap.

His head came through the other side then suddenly he was stuck, arms pinned to his sides. The rock above felt as though it was crushing down, restricting his breathing and the panic he had kept under tight control broke free. As mindless terror broke over him he kicked with his feet, but only succeeded in jamming himself even tighter.

He was going to die!

The thought filled his mind with tormented pictures as claustrophobia clawed at his reason. He heard hoarse screams of fear punch at his ears as stinging, blinding sweat rolled into his eyes and itched like ants on his scalp. It took him a few minutes to realize that the screams were his own and he forced himself to check them. He thought of dead Ben and the sisters that needed his help and he gradually brought his mind and body under control and forced himself to relax, the thudding of his heart loud in his ears. He took a shuddering breath and felt the rock squeeze his chest. Licking bone-dry lips he expelled the air from his lungs, felt the squeezing sensation release its grip and pushed again with his heels. This time he moved a couple of inches. He wriggled his shoulders and moved again. Pausing he took a few shallow breaths, expelled them and wriggled forward a few more inches.

The upper part of his body came through and he managed to drag his right arm clear aided by the narrowing space to his right. A few minutes later he dragged his legs clear, crawled a few yards and collapsed, dragging lungfuls of air in. His shoulders were rubbed raw where the hard floor had worn his sweat-soaked shirt away, but the pain was soothed away by the joy of being free.

After a few moments he rose into a half-crouch that was all the height of the tunnel permitted, buckled on his gunbelt and gathered up his coat and moved forward. The light had grown stronger from ahead coming from beyond a bend.

The air was cooler now, but his hopes of easy freedom were dashed as he rounded the bend and almost fell into the gaping jaws of a vertical shaft that plunged down into a stygian blackness. The shaft also rose above the tunnel and it was from here, an opening some thirty feet up, that a finger of golden sunlight speared through and splashed against the opposite wall of the shaft.

Matt stared up glumly feeling his former joy evaporate. The walls of the shaft were smooth and offered no way to reach the opening. With a weary groan he sank down on the edge of the tunnel and stared up at the tantalizing light.

The shaft was some ten-to-twelve feet across: the

result of water erosion in the far distant past when the mountain was young; water tumbling through the living rock, forming the shaft. In time the source of the water had dried up or found another path. Now it was just a dry shaft that led to nowhere. The 'Devil's Hole' that Pappy Duke had spoken of. Escape was there, but out of reach.

Matt awoke with a start unaware until that moment that he had fallen asleep. Sunlight no longer poked its inquisitive golden finger through the high opening. The light was dull and Matt realized that night was coming. He crawled away from the edge and hunkered down by the rock-fall pulling his coat on against the chill that was now creeping up the shaft.

He spent the night drifting in and out of troubled dozes, the cold gnawing into his bones and by the time dawn began filtering through the opening his body was stiff and cold. His teeth chattered and joints ached painfully as he climbed to his feet. He had to get his circulation going and so spent the next ten minutes doing press-ups and slowly bringing life back into his body. When he had warmed up enough, he returned to the shaft and studied it.

It was not as smooth as he had first supposed. There were small outcrops and the dark lines of cracks decorating the surface. As Matt viewed it a desperate plan grew in his mind, a plan that brought him out in a cold sweat. Squeezing beneath the rock-fall had been bad enough, but this was worse. But then he had nothing to lose but his life and that was forfeit anyway if he stayed put.

He would have to climb the wall of the shaft to reach the opening!

There were numerous cracks and ridges that made the feat possible and a long drop to eternity if he made a mistake. He stared a while longer at the walls of the shaft knowing that it was now or never. Without food or water his strength would rapidly deteriorate, making the proposed climb impossible. He undid the leg-tie of the holster and turned the gunbelt so the holster rested against his buttocks and would not snag.

The opening, high and right, suddenly appeared to be a long way off. Matt examined the wall of the shaft to the right of the tunnel, found toe and fingerholds and eased himself out into the shaft, turning his head in the direction he was going. With his heart in his mouth he clung to the wall of the shaft trying not to think of the drop below him, but his mind had a morbid fascination with it. Inch by inch he eased away from the tunnel sliding hands to the next hold and scraping at the wall with his feet until he found a hold.

It was a hard, punishing process. His fingers and shoulders ached and legs cried out for rest, but rest would only come if and when he reached the opening. His main worry was if the opening was not large enough. It was large enough on the inside, but he had not been able to see through. The outside of the opening could be only a few inches wide. If that was the case then . . . He did not like to dwell on the consequences, for there was no way he'd be able to return to the tunnel.

The distance between him and the opening decreased. Thirty feet had diminished to twenty and twenty to ten. His breathing was harsh and laboured. His palms sweated. Once his feet slipped and he hung there, fingertips hooked over a tiny ledge no more than half a fingernail wide while the darkness below beckoned. He managed to find purchase for his toes and continued. The opening came nearer and finally his left hand clamped itself over its edge. The right quickly followed and he hauled himself in to what was no more than a wide crack in the rock some three foot by two foot with an opening to the outside as wide as the inside. Hardly believing his luck, he crawled forward and stuck his head out, his flaring nostrils sucking in the scent of pine drifting up from far below. A few feet below him ran a wide shelf of rock. He levered himself out and collapsed on the rock, drawing sweet air into his lungs and letting his aching muscles relax. It was some moments before he sat up and took notice of his surroundings.

The rock shelf was in the shade facing west. High above, a crown of ragged pinnacles was backlit by the sun that would not move around to light up the opening until the afternoon. Far below him lay the deep pine forests and rolling hills painted with golden sunlight. An inquisitive breeze chilled his heated flesh and tugged at his clothes. He welcomed its cool touch. For a second time the Dukes had failed to kill him and he made up his mind there would not be a third attempt.

It was close to midday when, tired and exhausted,

Matt found his way back to the slope where buzzards fought over the decomposing bodies. From there it was a short haul to reach the clearing where Jethro and he had tethered the horses so long ago. The horses were still there. The big bay whickered a greeting at Matt and Matt smiled through dry, cracked lips.

'Horse, you're one helluva sight,' he croaked, staggering forward to retrieve the canteen and much-needed water. Matt used precious time after slaking his thirst to fix himself some food to replenish his lost strength.

It was late in the afternoon when he finally rode clear of the foothills and into the desert flats skirting the mountains. He had ridden fast and even now kept the pace up as much as he dared, to make up for lost time. The other horse he trailed behind on a line in case he needed it.

The sun was dipping towards the west when he mounted a ridge and saw the group of riders below him. He reined the bay to a snorting halt. He counted ten riders. One wore a badge, for it glinted on his check vest. He looked vaguely familiar. Matt kneed the bay forward down the slope towards them. Maybe his luck had changed at last. As he neared the waiting group he recognized the man wearing the star as Sheriff Crow from Larkinsville. The group formed a rough half-circle.

'Sheriff. Am I glad to see you,' Matt called out as he rode up.

'Not half as glad as I am to see you, son,' the heavy-set lawman responded as Matt came to a halt.

'We've got to get to the Sisters of Mercy Mission. The Dukes are riding on it and what they've got in mind ain't along the lines of the Good Book.'

The grim stares of the men began to filter into Matt's brain.

'Ain't the Dukes I'm looking for,' Crow said. 'You'll do.' He hauled iron as he spoke and suddenly Matt found himself covered by nine more rifles and the half-circle became a full circle with him at its centre. 'Raise your hands, son, or we'll kill you here and now.'

'What the hell's going on, sheriff?' Matt demanded.

'Catching ourselves a fugitive,' Crow replied. 'Walt, relieve Mr Holder of his guns.'

Matt could do nothing as a thin, skull-faced man moved forward and took his pistol and rifle.

'I'm no fugitive, sheriff,' Matt objected.

'You are now. Put your hands down and behind you back. Walt, cuff him.'

'Sheriff, you're making a mistake,' Matt protested as the skinny Walt cuffed his wrists.

'You made the mistake, Holder, by coming back.'

'Will you at least tell me what I'm supposed to have done?'

Sheriff Crow eyed him from beneath his hat brim.

'You sure are a cool one, but that won't help you now. You killed the Larkins boys and for that you're gonna hang.'

TEN

Darkness had settled over Larkinsville. In the confines of the cell with its single, blanketless bed and dirty, stained mattress that stank of sweat and vomit, Matt listened to the sounds of the night that drifted through the tiny, barred window above the bed.

He could hear the tinkle of an out-of-tune piano coming from the saloon that lay to the right of the jail. Distant voices raised in greeting. The drum of hoofbeats approaching and passing.

Matt sat on the noisome bed. His coat, gunbelt and boots had been removed and the stone floor was cold to his stockinged feet. He was still stunned at his arrest and protests of his innocence fell on deaf ears.

'It's for the circuit judge to decide,' was all Sheriff Crow would say as he had locked Matt into the cell. 'He'll be here in a couple of days.'

Since being locked up, Matt had been left alone, the only occupant of the small, double cell-block behind the sheriff's office. The two cage-like cells occupied the length of one side wall, their tiny, barred windows overlooking a narrow alley. A pair of oil lamps, suspended over the wide area that fronted the cells, threw their lambent, shadowy gloom over him. Nobody was interested in what he had to say. They listened with indifference and ignored him.

Muffled voices came through the closed door leading to the sheriff's office, then the door flew open and Abe Larkins, followed by the sheriff, entered. The old man marched up to the bars and stared, hollow-eyed, at Matt, the lines of grief carved deep into the flesh of his features.

'First their pa and now them.' There was anguish in his eyes. He gripped the bars with knuckle-whitened hands. 'Why did you have to kill them, Holder? I gave you money to get away from here. Why didn't you?' The bars rattled in the old man's trembling grip.

Matt rose, pushing his silver-spliced hair from his eyes.

'I didn't kill them, Mr Larkins. I never saw them again after I left town. They were killed by the Dukes.'

'Very convenient,' Abe sneered. 'Someone pees on the sidewalk and the Dukes get the blame. Not this time, Holder. You killed my boys, now you're gonna pay,' Abe Larkins shouted.

Matt was shocked by the old man's vehemence. From his brief meeting with Abe Larkins, Matt had sized him up as a man who thought first and acted second. Grief had turned that around.

'Your boys offered the Dukes $500 to kill me. I got that from Pappy Duke when he bragged about killing them.'

'It won't work, Holder.' The old man grinned and stepped back from the bars. 'You're pretty fast with a gun and the sheriff here tells me you got the marks of leg irons. Former Yuma inmate, I reckon. Figure you to have followed the boys and finished the job off I stopped you from doing on a previous occasion.' The man was adamant in his belief and Matt felt a sick feeling in the pit of his stomach. It was his turn now to grip the bars.

'The sisters at the Mission are in danger. Send men out there now. The Dukes are going to kill them and worse,' Matt begged, but Abe Larkins eyed him stonily.

'The Dukes, the Dukes,' Abe raved throwing his arms about in anger. 'The way it's coming out you seem a mite friendly with the Dukes. They tell you things and let you live. That ain't their style, mister.'

'They tried before in the desert,' Matt replied. 'And again in the mountains.'

'And they failed again?' There was incredulity in the old man's voice. 'Mister, you're pitching a line that's gonna make sure the noose goes round your neck. I'll tell you something, mister.' He poked his chest, leering at Matt. 'I don't believe the Dukes played any part in this, 'cepting in your imagination. You're using them to cover up your own crimes.' He glared at Matt. 'Have the Dukes been heard of in the area, sheriff?' His eyes did not leave Matt.

Sheriff Luke Crow smiled. He wore his paunch like a badge of office, proudly.

'Not a whisper, Mr Larkins,' he drawled. 'Last I heard they were over Mexico way an' that was six months ago.' The sheriff smirked.

'You won't be able to lie your way out of this, Holder,' the old man said. 'You'll hang when the circuit judge gets here in two days time. I've sent a wire to the governor of Yuma Prison. I reckon I'll have all the answers I need by the time Judge Wilkes gets here.'

'By that time the sisters at the Mission will be dead,' Matt said darkly. 'It'll be on your conscience, old man, and your's, sheriff.'

'Set me right on one thing, Holder. Why should the Dukes bother with a pack of holy women?' Abe Larkins asked.

'Because I shot Billy Duke a couple of days ago at a place called Mountain Bend.'

'That den of thieves,' Sheriff Crow exclaimed. 'Ain't no place for a decent man. What was you doing there?'

'Looking to kill Dukes. Pappy Duke blames the sister for the death of Billy. He reckons if they had not saved me then Billy would be alive now.'

'Happen that could be right,' Sheriff Crow agreed, earning himself a black look from Matt.

'How come they didn't kill you for killing Billy?' Abe Larkins asked.

'They tried,' Matt said. 'Walled me up in a mountain cave. Damn near brought the roof down on my head, but I got out.'

'Seems you get out of too many things, Holder,' Abe Larkins sneered. 'But this is one you won't get out of. You killed Tom and Dan and if it wasn't for a prospector wandering the foothills, their bodies might never have been found and you'd have been free and clear. We start building the gallows tomorrow so it'll be ready by the time the judge arrives.'

'You're making a terrible mistake, old man,' Matt shouted angrily, shaking the bars. 'I never killed your boys and there's going to be six dead women if you don't get some men to the Mission.'

The old man ignored his plea.

'I'll enjoy seeing you swinging at the end of a rope, Matt Holder. We ain't had a hanging in Larkinsville for twenty years or more. Ain't that right, Crow?'

'Sure is, Mr Larkins.'

'And it's going to make an old man very happy,' Abe Larkins concluded. He looked at Crow. 'Make sure he's well fed and watered, sheriff. We want him fit and healthy on the day he swings.' Abe Larkins turned away and marched to the door followed by Sheriff Crow.

'Send men to the Mission, Larkins. Don't let anything happen to those women . . . .'

The door slammed and once again he was on his own.

During the next day Seth Coggins came to see him. Seth stared at the ragged, dirty figure in the cell.

'Hell, son. You look like you done be run over by a stampede.'

Matt smiled at the man.

'Would have been easier if'n I had.' He cocked his head to one side. 'Folks seem a mite busy outside.' He made reference to the hammering and sawing he could hear from outside.

'Damn fools. Any one'd think it was a holiday coming up, not a hanging. Did yer kill the Larkins, Matt?' Seth's eyes caught and held his.

'What do you think?' Matt asked quietly.

'I think no, but I ain't the one that matters. Abe Larkins figures it was you, so the town figures the same. The circuit judge is a friend of Abe's.'

'So I haven't got a chance in hell?'

'Sorry, son,' Seth said softly, a dejected look on his lined face.

'There's nothing for you to be sorry for, Seth. It's the sisters that need the help and it may be too late for them already.'

Sheriff Crow wandered in, smiling.

'Reckon your time's up, Seth, though why you bother with this no-account I ain't figured.'

'The boy didn't do it. You fetched the bodies in. Dan was back-shot, big calibre and Tom took a .45 slug. Matt here carries a .44.'

'Ain't no problem using different guns, old man, and getting rid of 'em afterwards. Anyway, how do you know? You weren't there.'

'Heared the men talking,' Seth said defensively.

'Could be you heard wrong. Now git on back to the livery and let this boy contemplate his sins.'

'Here, I brung you something.' Seth finished a couple of stogies and matches from a pocket and handed them through the bars to Matt.

'Here. What's going on?' Crow pulled his gun and relaxed when he saw the smokes, but his tone was belligerent with Seth. 'Ain't allowed to give prisoners things. I oughta lock you up.'

'You should be out to the Mission,' Seth shot back. 'If'n the Dukes are there it'll back up the boy's story.'

'And if'n they ain't it's a long, hot ride for nothing. Now git on back to your horses, old man, afore I lose patience.'

'Take care, Seth. You and Clara,' Matt called.

'I'll get your evidence, son,' Seth said. 'I'll do your work for you, sheriff, seeing as you ain't got time.'

'Get out, old man, and sit in your rocker,' Crow said.

'Seth. Don't go doing anything stupid,' Matt called anxiously after him and Seth turned in the doorway.

'Sit tight, son. You ain't hanging without a fight. I can get there and back by tomorrow afternoon.'

Another night passed and during the next day Matt waited anxiously for news of Seth. Come nightfall of the second day Seth had not returned. The only news that Matt received was that Judge Wilkes had arrived in town.

Matt did not get much sleep that night. There seemed to be a carnival spirit in town. People were out enjoying themselves, getting ready for tomorrow's entertainment.

The following morning Sheriff Crow did not bother to get him any breakfast, only a cup of lukewarm coffee.

'Ain't no good wasting good food on a corpse,' he said.

It was about ten o' clock when Matt was taken from the cell, through a throng of jeering bystanders, to the saloon where the court was to be held. The

tables had been cleared back and one set up in front
of the bar where a heavily moustached man in a dark
suit sat, black hair slickered back over a balding
head. He was deep in conversation with Abe Larkins, but his deep-set eyes drifted indolently to Matt
as he was brought in and made to stand in a cleared
area before him. Matt's boots had been returned to
him and his tattered, dirty shirt had been replaced by
a clean, white one, courtesy of the town. Matt was
flanked on one side by Sheriff Crow and a deputy on
the other. To the right, twelve men lounged in chairs
set out in two rows of six. They had the look of
rangemen about them. Larkin's men, and they
formed the jury.

Matt returned the look with a stony stare as people
crowded into the saloon forming a wide half-circle,
four or five deep, to view the proceedings. The man,
obviously Judge Wilkes, looked away. It was some
minutes before the conversation between the two
broke up and Abe Larkins moved to a table to one
side of the judge. The buzz of conversation continued unabated until Judge Wilkes pulled a .45 and
fired a shot into the air. Women squealed, but it had
the desired effect and a hush settled through the
saloon.

'The bar is closed. Court is now in session,' Wilkes
roared in a gravel-throated rasp. 'Judge Eugene
Wilkes presiding.' His fierce, dark eyes travelled
around the makeshift court before settling on Matt.
'Matthew Holder, you are up before this court for
the callous murder of Tom and Dan Larkins. How
do you plead?'

'Does it matter?' Matt replied.

'Answer properly, boy, or you'll be in contempt of this court.'

Matt let his eyes drift around and a smile tugged at his lips.

'Not guilty.'

A jeer went up around the bar and the 'jury' laughed.

'Silence in court,' Wilkes roared, coming to his feet and rapping the butt of the .45 on the table-top. The crowd quietened. Wilkes moved out from behind the table and swaggered forward to stand before Matt. He was a head shorter than Matt. He gripped the lapels of his own coat.

'I'm judge and prosecutor. Who speaks for you, boy?'

'I speak for myself.'

'Good. Now in my position as prosecutor I shall lay the evidence before the court of this man's guilt.'

'What evidence?' Matt demanded.

Wilkes drew a telegram from his pocket and waved it about.

'This here's a telegram from the governor of Yuma prison.' He stared hard at Matt. 'Says you spent five years there for killing a man in a fast-draw shootout. Evidence you're good with a gun, Mr Holder. Mr Larkins here will testify, if called upon, that if he hadn't arrived in time a coupla weeks back, you would have killed Tom Larkins. We also have written statements from a number of witnesses that you accused the Larkins boys of holding up the stage and thereby causing unnecessary aggravation to the boys.

In short, Mr Holder, I state that you, a convicted gunman, took a dislike to the Larkins boys and deliberately goaded them into a situation that had not Mr Larkins happened upon it, you would have killed the boys there and then.'

Matt was stunned.

'That's not true at all.'

'Can you call up a witness to testify otherwise?'

'Seth Coggins at the livery.'

'He's outta town, Judge,' Sheriff Crow said.

'No witnesses,' Wilkes thundered. 'Isn't it true that Mr Larkins gave you $500 to get out of town and leave his boys alone?'

'It wasn't like that,' Matt said weakly.

'Did he or did he not give you the aforementioned money?'

'Yes.'

'Evidence enough,' Wilkes cried out. He had been strutting back and forth all the time he had been speaking, now he halted before Matt. 'It's called circumstantial evidence and it's weighed real heavy against you. No one see'd you kill those poor boys, but you're a known gunslick and killer. You come into town and a few days later two fine young citizens are dead.'

'The Dukes killed them.'

'It's convenient to have someone else to blame, Mr Holder. But in my experience gunslicks like yourself have to follow through with their threats or lose a reputation. I see it all the time.'

'That's nonsense,' Matt said, but people all around were nodding their heads in agreement with the judge.'

'What have you got to say in your defence?' Wilkes asked.

Matt looked across at the grinning jury members.

'Somehow I don't think it'll make much difference to the outcome whatever I say.'

'The accused has nothing to say. I therefore rest my case and pronounce Matt Holder guilty,' Wilkes roared at the jury.

'When do we git to vote?' A voice called from the jury.

'All in good time, son.' Wilkes returned to his seat.

'In my capacity as judge I now ask you members of the jury for a show of hands. Raise your hands for guilty.' Twelve hands shot into the air. 'Unanimous agreement.' He looked at Matt. 'Guilty as sin, boy and that just leaves the sentence.' A silence settled through the room. 'You're to be hung by the neck until you're dead, boy. The good folk of Larkinsville don't tolerate gunslicks. The sentence to be carried out at twelve noon precisely. Court adjourned. Open the bar.'

A ragged cheer went up as Matt was hustled away back to his cell to spend the final hour. He hoped as he sat there that Seth would return, but he doubted that the old man would even be listened too. A farcical court procedure had been carried out that had nothing to do with justice. Just a proceedings to legalize his murder.

Seth had still not returned by the time Matt was led from the jail and out to the gallows that had been erected in the middle of Main Street just for him. The sunlight caught the naked wood and it shone with a faint, golden aura. Matt's legs felt like lead as he mounted the wooden steps, hands roped behind his back. He stumbled twice before he reached the platform. He was guided onto the trap by the burly blacksmith who had won the job of hangman for the day on a draw of cards. The noose was slipped over his head and tightened. Matt refused to give in to the fear that jellied his brain and give the half-circle of waiting people the pleasure of seeing him plead. Sheriff Crow took up a position to Matt's right. The blacksmith moved to the left and settled his great hands on the lever that would operate the trap beneath Matt's feet.

Abe Larkins came up onto the platform and stood before Matt.

'I reckon my boys will rest easier now,' he said softly.

'You never will again, old man, when they find those sisters massacred and realize that I have been speaking the truth.'

'Keeping the false innocence going to the end, eh? You're guilty, boy, and justice is being done.' He nodded to the blacksmith. He moved to the edge of Matt's vision and a sweat of fear oozed from the pores of his body.

A shot rang out. The blacksmith gave a cry and staggered back clutching a shoulder that spouted blood. Women screamed and men shouted and next to him Sheriff Crow mumbled, 'Hell shit!' Matt snapped his closed eyes open and gaped in amazement. In the centre of Main Street, astride tough, wiry pintos, sat the imposing form of the Apache chief, Running Fox, and his son, Red Cloud. Both carried rifles and by the smoking barrel it had been Running Fox that had fired.

The two Apaches kneed their horses forward.

'Look up, white eyes,' Running Fox's voice boomed out. 'Should the one called Matt Holder die, then all will die.'

Matt looked up as others did. On every surrounding rooftop stood an Apache with a rifle, ready, should Running Fox give the signal. Sheriff Crow's face had grown white.

'No!' Abe Larkins shouted, darted forward and pulled the lever.

Matt heard the click of the release mechanism and felt himself falling.

ELEVEN

Matt felt a surge of fear wash through him as he dropped, waiting to hear the snap of his neck as he reached the limit of the rope. It did not come. Instead the rope tightened on his neck as he came to an abrupt halt on his downward plummet. Neck muscles screeched their agony as they took the full weight of his body. The rope gripped his throat like a band of iron as he hung there, turning slowly, face shading to purple. A roaring noise filled his ears overlaid with the drumming of his heart and the ominous creak of neck bones stretching. The pain coupled with the slow strangulation made his body jerk and kick. The position of the taut rope at the back of his head locked his head in the forward position. All he could see through blurred and darkening vision was the rough boards that made up the deep body of the gallows.

Suddenly he was falling again, the awful pulling, stretching pressure gone, but the strangling grip remained. He hit the ground feeling coils of the rope tumbling about him. With his hands roped behind him he could not reach the noose to loosen it. He was vaguely aware of a figure thumping down beside him. Hands tore the rope from his throat and cut his wrists free. Matt was not interested in who or how at that precise moment as he drew shuddering breaths into his starved lungs, the effort causing him to cough and choke. When he was able to take an interest, Red Cloud was helping him to his feet.

'I don't know where you sprung from, Red Cloud, but I'm mighty glad to see you,' Matt croaked in a harsh whisper, massaging his throat.

'Yellow Hand saw your capture by the white eyes and told Running Fox. It was then agreed in council to take you from the white eyes.'

'I'm more'n glad you did.' Matt cast his eyes around and up and shuddered. 'Let's get out of here.'

Emerging through the doors that normally the undertaker took his casket in by, Matt found the townsfolk surrounding the gallows surrounded themselves by a ring of stone-faced Apaches. Running Fox kneed his mount forward.

'It is good you live, Matt Holder.'

'I'm quite pleased about that myself,' Matt admitted.

'Why do they do this?' Running Fox demanded.

'The Dukes,' Matt spat. 'They killed that old man's grandsons.' Matt indicated Abe Larkins gripping the rail above. 'And I got the blame. Right now the Dukes are riding on the Sisters of Mercy Mission and I need to get there quick.'

'We ride with you,' Running Fox intoned. 'The Apaches too have waited too long to avenge themselves on the ones called Dukes.'

'I'd be proud to have you along,' Matt said. Leaving the Apaches to hold the frightened crowd in check, Matt retrieved his gunbelt, hat and coat from the jail. He had three horses plus his own bay saddled by a rattled deputy and then had Larkins, Wilkes and Sheriff Crow brought over.

'What's going on, Holder?' Wilkes demanded.

'We're all going on a little trip,' Matt replied grimly. 'Now mount up, all of you.'

'I'm not going anywhere,' Abe Larkins said defiantly.

'Mr Larkins. You accused me of killing your boys. You almost had me hung for it. Now I'm going to give you the chance of meeting the real killers. Get on that horse or I'll have you tied on it.' Matt's eyes flashed. Abe Larkins remained defiant for a few seconds more, then his defiance fled and in silence he mounted to join the waiting Wilkes and Crow.

The Apaches had come down from their rooftop perches and, save for half a dozen still ringing the crowd, were mounted behind Running Fox and Red Cloud. No attempt had been made to disarm the men in the crowd, but none had reached for their weapons. The legendary fierceness of the Apaches giving them a bout of good sense. Matt reined his bay close to the crowd as Running Fox ordered the last of his men to mount — they numbered about twenty in all — and addressed the crowd.

'I intend to prove that I had nothing to do with the deaths of Tom and Dan Larkins. The judge, sheriff and Larkins are going to be my witnesses. We will be riding to the Sisters of Mercy Mission. I'd advise against any action that might cause the deaths of these three men. In case you feel like getting a message to the cavalry, remember that if any attempt is made to stop us, you'll be three citizens short. I personally will make sure of that. If they are not back in three days then by all means get the cavalry, because that means we are all dead.' With that speech delivered Matt kneed the bay forward and a few moments later he and the band of Apaches thundered from the town, heading north-west to the Mission. They had seventy miles to cover, at normal speed a two-day journey. Matt intended to reduce that to hours. It meant running the horses near their limit in the heat of the desert, but he wanted to reach the Mission before nightfall, although a bad gut feeling told him it was too late.

No words were spoken for the next four hours as the flying hooves of the sweating horses ate up the miles. To the west, the ridge of mountains were blue hazed and distant. They rode across a vast, yellow, semi-arid plain dotted with mesquite and scrub and stands of tall, green saguaro cactus. It was late afternoon by the time they reached the way-station at Desert Rock and Matt knew that his gut feeling had not been wrong.

The way-station had not been much of a place, now it was even less. All that remained of it was a blackened, charred heap with a few ribs of char-coaled timber rising out of the aches here and there. Buzzards flapped about the carcasses of three dead horses in the corral. Amid the ruins Matt found the

burnt, flesh-boiled remains of the station manager
and the Mexican hostler. The acrid taint of burnt
wood and flesh still hung thick in the air.

'Two days, mebbe,' Running Fox said impassively
as he crumbled ash in his hand after joining Matt.
Matt nodded and turned away to face Abe Larkins
who was still mounted, fury leaping in his eyes.

'The Dukes have been here. I told you,' he grated
harshly.

'This don't prove nothing,' Larkins snapped back.
His back and buttocks hurt from the hard ride.
'Could'a been an accident. Place like this, dry as
tinder . . . .'

Without a word Matt reached up and pulled the
man roughly from the saddle. Abe yelped as pain
laced through his legs and back. His legs almost gave
out under him from being so long in one position as
Matt pushed him forward into the burnt-out ruins
and indicated the two spread-eagled figures on what
had once been the floor of the station.

'Sure, the two nailed themselves to the floor so
they wouldn't get blown away,' Matt snarled. 'Take
a good look, old man.' The six inch nails that had
been driven through the hands and feet of the two
corpses were plain to see.

Abe Larkins eyes opened in revulsion.

'Could'a been Indians,' he mumbled weakly.

A cold smile touched Matt's eyes.

'Have a care, old man,' he hissed warningly. Abe
Larkins swallowed uneasily as he caught Running
Fox's hard glare. 'Let's get to the Mission,' Matt
concluded huskily.

Seth Coggins jerked awake as the drumming of
hooves shook the ground. The movement shook a
blanket of flies loose from his blood-soaked shirt-
front and they buzzed angrily about his head. He sat
against a rock, legs stretched out before him, getting
temporary shade from a stand of saguaro as the sun
moved behind him. He tried to reach the butt of a
pistol sticking up from the sand. The effort raised a
bubbling moan in his throat and blood spilled from
his mouth. The hoof-beats grew louder. He tried
harder, leaning forward, but the effort was too
much. He toppled sideways onto the sand. The rock
where his back had rested was bright red with blood.

Matt saw the horse first to the left of the faint trail,
standing in the shade of a saguaro stand. It pricked
up its ears and whickered at their approach. Matt's
eyes swept around and settled on the crumpled form
by a second saguaro stand to the right of the trail. He
swept towards it, reining the bay to a slithering halt
and leaping off.

'Seth.' He turned the man gently and cradled his
head in his arms. Seth's eyes flickered open. They
were filled with pain.

'Did they let you go, son?' his voice was a dry
whisper.

'Sort of.' Matt brushed sand from the old man's
face. 'What happened to you?'

'The Dukes. They were at the Mission.' Seth
coughed. Red Cloud came across with a canteen and
handed it wordlessly to Matt who dribbled a little of
the water on to the old man's lips. Matt's insides had

grown cold at the news. 'They damn well shot me all to hell,' Seth continued. 'Had to get help.' His eyes flickered onto Red Cloud and popped a little. 'Injuns, Matt.' He grabbed at Matt's arm.

'He's a friend,' Matt soothed. 'Are they still at the Mission?'

'I don't know, son. It was just afore dark they got me. Guess that was yesterday.' His body convulsed in a coughing spasm and fresh blood dribbled from his lips. The skin of his face had grown waxen while the eyes swam in gaunt hollows. Death was reaching out for the old man. 'Tried to get back,' he mumbled.

'You did good, Seth.'

'Clara, my Clara! Who's gonna look after my Clara?' Tears welled in the dying man's eyes and his grip tightened on Matt's arm.

'She'll be taken care of. You've got my word on that,' Matt promised and Seth smiled.

'Ain't too bright, but she ain't stupid. Tell her I love her.' Seth's head lolled to one side and the hand relinquished its grip and flopped in the sand.

Matt lowered the head gently and stood up, rage burning in his eyes. He said nothing as he pulled a blanket from his bed-roll and covered the old man.

'I'll be back for you, old-timer,' he promised, and returned to his horse. Minutes later the group thundered on towards the Mission.

The last time Matt had cried was on the day he returned to the desert to find the pecked-clean bones of his son Ben. He cried again as he stood within the Mission walls an hour later. He had thought that nothing else could touch him, hurt him, but the sight of the six dead, naked, violated bodies strewn about the inner courtyard, brought the tears. Death had been brought about by either a bullet between the eyes or the throat slit with a knife. But it had been a long death for each of them, that had begun the moment the Dukes raped them.

The tears flooded hotly down his cheeks, blurring his vision. He knelt at the side of the mother superior and drew her torn, ragged garments over her nakedness.

'I'm sorry.' The words fell brokenly from his trembling lips as he remembered her prophetic words when they parted. "Revenge can hurt the innocent as well as the guilty".

Matt knuckled the tears from his eyes. In the rose corner the earth over Ben's grave had been turned and fresh flowers placed there. He drew in a deep, shuddering breath and climbed to his feet. His eyes, as they raked hotly across the three men, struck each like a physical blow.

The Indians stood in silence beyond the gaping hole where once strong, double wooden doors had stood. Dynamite had blown the doors to splinters and taken a section of wall away.

Matt's gaze fastened on Abe Larkins' white, shocked face. He strode forward and grabbed two fistfuls of coat-front.

'You did this, old man.' His voice shook with suppressed rage. 'You were so anxious to hang me for the deaths of your grandsons, that you wouldn't listen when I said the sisters were in danger.' He threw the old man forward sending him down on his knees by a dead sister. 'Take a real good look, Larkins. You'll never sleep a peaceful night again.'

'I didn't know,' the old man wailed, scrambling to his feet. 'How could I?'

'Because I told you, old man. I told you.' Matt wheeled away and faced the sheriff. The man took a step back, but not far enough to avoid the vicious back-hand blow that Matt threw. It slapped hard against the sheriff's mouth, staggering him back further and drawing blood from a split lip.

'How does it feel to know that you could have prevented this, Crow?' Matt snarled.

'You don't know that.' Crow knuckled blood from his lip.

'I asked you to get men out here and you laughed at the idea.'

'You were an arrested killer. Don't send men riding into the desert on a killer's word,' Crow said flatly.

'Arrested, but not convicted, except in that man's mind and you ran with him and made me guilty. Tell me, Crow, who's gonna arrest you for your part in the murder of these women? Because you're as guilty as the old man.' He eyed Wilkes. 'And how about you, judge?'

'I'm no part of this circus,' Wilkes protested. 'I'm new in town.'

'You're as guilty as them, judge. In your eyes I was already a dead man in that so-called court of yours. Convicted before I was even tried. Circumstantial evidence. You weren't interested in getting at the truth. No, Judge, you're not blameless. If I'd have hung then this would have been blamed on the Indians.'

'Maybe I cut corners to aid the course of justice, but what's happened here don't prove that you didn't kill the Larkins boys.'

'The important point is that you couldn't prove I did.' The Schofield-Smith and Wesson appeared in Matt's hand. His eyes were hard and unrelenting. 'Maybe I should put a bullet in your head now, judge, and save future innocent people from being hung just because you happen to be friendly with the accusing party.' The hammer clicked back ominously and Wilkes' face became pastry-white.

'Now wait a minute.' Wilkes held out his hands.

'Don't worry, judge.' Matt put up the weapon and returned it to its holster. 'I aim to provide the evidence that you couldn't be bothered to find out. In the meantime six graves have got to be dug. You and the other two have been elected. Anyone want to argue about it?' His eyes swept the three, but no one said anything. 'Good. You'll find spades in a shed around back. 'Crow, you get 'em.'

Running Fox came across to Matt.

'We find horse droppings. Two, maybe three, hours old and the tracks of three horses heading west. I have sent Red Cloud and two braves to follow the tracks. It will be dark soon. The Dukes will make camp for the night. Red Cloud will return and tell us where.'

Matt nodded.

'Obliged, Running Fox. They're not going to get

away this time.'

It was nightfall by the time the last of the bodies was buried, Matt tenderly wrapping each body in a blanket. It was a harrowing business and later, as darkness fell proper, he found a half-full bottle of whiskey in one of the small sleeping cells in the mission. He presumed it had been left by the Dukes.

Each of the tiny rooms had been systematically wrecked, spartan furniture smashed and personal belongings scattered in wanton destruction. In one room Matt found a stick of dynamite that had been dropped by one of the Dukes.

With a lantern Matt wandered like some huge firefly from one room to the other. It was in the tiny altar at the rear of the Mission that he found evidence that could prove his innocence in the deaths of the Larkins boys. He gathered it up and returned outside.

The Apaches had camped outside the Mission and behind a clump of brush had built a small fire. Matt found the three men huddled together just within the shattered doorway. They looked up as Matt approached, the lantern throwing moving shadows ahead and behind as it swung in his hand.

'Here!' He threw something at Abe Larkins. The old man caught it in a reflex action. It was a yellow silk bandanna and in one corner, as the old man unfolded it, were the initials, T.L. 'Recognize it?' he queried.

'It's Tom's . . . was Tom's. Where did you get it?'

'I found it inside. I guess one of the Dukes dropped it.' Matt put the lamp at their feet and walked out to where Running Fox was hunkered over the fire where a jack-rabbit sizzled on a stick. Matt threw himself down wearily and leaned his back against a rock, rubbing his eyes.

'You are tired, my friend,' Running Fox observed.

'Some, I guess. It's been a long haul.' The flames played with shadows on his face and sparkled in his eyes. The darkness pressed around the tiny glow. Overhead the stars scattered with careless abandon across the velvet of the night, winked and shivered. 'I came out here to start a new life and death has rode with me ever since. It won't be gone until the Dukes are dead.'

Running Fox tossed a haunch of rabbit across to him.

'Eat. Red Cloud will return when the Dukes are found. Until then strength must be maintained.' Running Fox rose up. 'The white eyes that came with you must eat also.'

'I guess you're right, Running Fox.'

'Share with them. I will return when Red Cloud comes with news.'

The Apache chief vanished into the night. Matt called the three to join him, even going to the extent of brewing coffee. It was later that Abe Larkins spoke to Matt.

'I've been doing a lot of thinking, Holder. Maybe I did get it wrong about you.' He glanced across to see Matt's reaction and saw bleak, grey eyes staring back at him from a grim, expressionless face. 'You gotta admit you came into town, argued with the boys and then they were found dead. It's a mighty strong argument against you.' If he was hoping for some sort of pleased relief from Matt he was due for a disappointment.

'I'm sure the Sisters of Mercy will get a real comfort from that, Larkins, in their graves.'

The old man flinched at the hard, unforgiving coldness in Matt's voice.

'I guess I deserved that,' Larkins admitted. 'But you ain't clear of their deaths, mister. If you hadn't come here in the first place none of this would have come about. You killed one Duke when you should'a killed them all. You left the others alive to avenge Billy.'

It was then that Matt knew what was gnawing on him so badly. It was not so much their guilt in the deaths of the sisters. It was his own.

TWELVE

The dawn mist turned the figures about Matt into grey, featureless ghosts. Behind Matt rode Larkins, Crow and Wilkes, the jingle and clink of harness rode the air with the snort of horses. The Indians came and went with apparent ease, seemingly unhampered by the mist.

Red Cloud had returned in the early hours of the morning leaving the two braves to keep a watch on the Dukes' camp. In the pre-dawn light a hasty breakfast was consumed before they began the final part of their journey in search of the Dukes.

Matt rode uneasy in the saddle, unable to explain the tension that gripped him. Maybe it was the unknown quality that the mist gave the land, hiding its treacheries and deceits until the second before disaster. Hiding the Dukes. In an hour or so the rising sun would have burnt the mist away and he would be able to see again and the feeling would pass.

It didn't!

As the sun opened up the landscape Matt's feeling of unease grew. The Dukes were only three, out-

numbered nine to one, yet . . . They were hard,
fearless men with the instinct and cunning of animals; and animals when cornered are at their most
dangerous. They had survived in the wild for so long
that they had become part of the wild. To destroy the
Dukes forever would not be an easy task, Matt
thought.

They moved at a steady canter across the vast,
ochre plain of rock, sand, seguaro and brush that
shimmered beneath a cobalt sky that spread to the
distant grey ridge of mountains. After an hour or so
the terrain began to change. The ochre became
yellow, the seguaro and scrub less. The ground grew
softer and opened onto a sea of dunes that rippled
away into the distance.

Red Cloud rode up alongside Matt.

'Soon we will be at their camp. Yellow Dog and
Leaping Deer are watching. Should the white eyes
leave, then Yellow Dog and Leaping Deer will
follow and leave signs for us.' With that he veered
away and rejoined his father. As a plan Matt could
find no fault with it. It all seemed so easy; too easy.

The horses floundered in the sand as their hooves
sunk. The heat closed in as they rode between the
high dunes. They emerged from the dunes thirty
minutes later as the terrain returned to seguaro and
scrub. A series of low hills rose ahead scattered with
stands of twisted oak and tangled thorn and soon
they were among them and reduced to single file as
the ground fell away into a steep-sided canyon.
Running Fox ordered silence, but the ring of saddle
harness coming from Matt's and the other three's

horses echoed and jingled happily from the walls. Where the canyon widened into a circular arena Running Fox brought the group to a halt, with a startled cry.

To the right, hidden until they entered the circle, a figure slumped in ropes that bound him to a dead oak stump. His head hung forward, chin on chest, long, dark hair held in place by a headband. Matt could see that it was an Indian and he heard Red Cloud cry out, 'Yellow Dog', and make as if to go forward, but Running Fox stopped him with a sharp command, dark eyes peering around restlessly. Matt felt the knot of unease tighten in his gut as his eyes searched the high rim of the canyon. Satisfied, Running Fox, with Red Cloud at his side, kneed his horse forward and Matt followed.

Red Cloud leaped from his pinto and approached the lolling figure, lifting the man's head. Matt felt his stomach rise to the back of his throat. The Indian's eyes had been gouged out to leave two blood-blackened holes. Dried blood ran a thick, encrusted trail from each empty socket. Running Fox eyed the dead, mutilated man with an impassiveness of face that did not match the rage that burned in his dark eyes. As Red Cloud let the head drop Running Fox drew an army-issue Spencer from a hide scabbard and wheeled his horse away, digging in with his heels and dragging on the reins. The pinto rose on its hind legs, pawing the air with its forelegs. A loud, keening whoop issued from the Indian's lips sending a stab of fear through Matt. He had heard such war cries before and was glad he was not on the end of it. The

Apache that had remained now surged forward and galloped to bunch about Running Fox who barked a series of guttural orders in his own tongue. Two men detached themselves from the group, left behind to tend the dead Indian. Two more returned to where the three men from Larkinsville waited. The rest grouped behind Running Fox as he galloped with Red Cloud to the far exit. Matt returned to where the three from Larkinsville waited.

'What the hell's going on, Holder?' Judge Wilkes demanded.

'The Dukes have killed one of Running Fox's men. Cut the poor bastard's eyes out,' Matt replied grimly. 'Let's go. Join up with Running Fox before he gets the idea that all white eyes are as bad as the Dukes.'

'Is he likely to do that?' Sheriff Crow asked, anxiously.

'Try riding the other way and find out,' Matt offered bleakly.

'This is your fault, Holder, making us come along,' Abe Larkins fumed.

'You got a short memory, Larkins. Seems to me that it's because of your accusations we're all here now. Let's ride.'

With Matt in the lead and the two Apaches bringing up the rear, the group galloped in the wake of Running Fox and his braves. The canyon walls closed about them and the thud of hooves echoed back and forth between the walls. Five minutes after entering the canyon and following its tortured, twisting route, they emerged into a steep valley where grey rock piles grew from the dry, ochre earth amid scrub-topped dusty hillocks. It looked like they were deep within the mountains for all around them sheer, grey precipices of rock rose to tear at the cobalt sky with ragged rims. Roughly circular, it was at least a mile wide, maybe more; a still, forgotten place in the heart of the mountains that nature had sculpted in secret. Deeper into the valley the rock formations became clusters of needle-pointed spires, some of which rose fifty feet into the air.

Running Fox and Red Cloud had dismounted from their pintos and were bent over a figure on the ground as Matt rode up. It was Leaping Deer, his still, sprawled body red with blood from dozens of cuts that criss-crossed the bronze skin, but these had not been the cause of his death. His torture had finally ended when his throat had been slashed open. Blood soaked the sand and stone ground about the body. Much of the blood was still wet and Matt figured silently that the Indian had died less than an hour since. He climbed down from the bay, rifle in hand.

'I'm sorry about your braves, Running Fox,' Matt said quietly.

'The Apache lives with death, Matt Holder, he does not fear it. The Dukes will pay dearly for this. They have entered the Valley of Spirits. The way in is also the way out. They cannot go further.' His words were accompanied by the distant roar of a gunshot that echoed about the enclosed valley. One of the cluster of mounted Indians to their left threw up his arms in a jerky fashion, his forehead exploding outwards as the bullet entering the back of his head made a gory exit and his body pitched to the ground.

'Sharps! Take cover!' Matt yelled, recognizing the distinctive sound of the powerful, single-shot weapon. A deadly weapon in the hands of an expert, with a range well in excess of a thousand yards: and Pappy Duke was an expert. Matt dived down behind a tumble of rocks, heart thumping as he rolled on to his back and levered a bullet into the breech of his Winchester. It was a token gesture, more to bring comfort than to be of use, for the Sharps greatly out-shot the Winchester. Sheriff Crow and Red Cloud thumped to the ground either side of him. There was a sporadic rattle of gunfire from the Indians, firing wildly in all directions.

'Jesus, Holder. I hear tell that Pappy Duke can shoot the balls off'n a fly at a thousand yards with a Sharps. He can pick us off one by one.' He was sweating and shaking.

'Don't worry, Crow, I aim to keep you and the others alive. If you die I'm up for murder. Just keep your head down.'

'Ain't needing no telling twice.'

Matt smiled thinly and looked at Red Cloud who was belly down, head almost on the ground, peering around the outer edge of the lowest boulder.

'Make out where it came from, Red Cloud?'

'To the west where many rock spears stand together,' Red Cloud said softly, eyes not leaving the spot. Matt came to his knees and found a place to peer between two boulders balanced on the shoulders of a third. It took a moment's hard staring but finally he located the spot. A high bluff of rock backed by a wall of stone spires. He was impressed, it was over half a mile away, perhaps three-quarters, he saw no movement or glint of sunlight on metal. Nothing to indicate that the Dukes, one of them at least, was holed up there; but he had no cause to doubt Red Cloud's eyes. It was also a view shared by Running Fox who started his braves forward, moving from rock to rock.

Judge Wilkes squirmed to Matt's side.

'Abe Larkins is in a bad shape, Holder. He may not make it.' Grimed with trail dust and dirt, he stared grimly at Holder who returned his gaze with puzzlement. A thin, mirthless smile touched Wilkes's face at the look. 'He's an old man,' he explained. 'He can't take what you've put him through.'

Without a word Matt moved to where Abe Larkins lay sprawled out behind some rocks, finding just enough shade for his head.

'Larkins?'

The old man's eyes flickered open in a face that was suddenly shrunken and white.

'Keeled over all of a sudden,' Wilkes, who had followed, said. 'You pushed him too hard, Holder.'

'Heart,' Larkins' voice fell in a dry whisper from his lips.

'How are you feeling?' There was genuine concern in Matt's voice. The object of the exercise had been to prove his innocence to the old man. Not kill him in the process.

'I've knowed it better, but I ain't aiming to die yet.' He struggled into a sitting position with Matt's help.

'We've gotta get him back to Larkinsville,' Wilkes pressed. 'This heat'll kill him for sure.'

'Don't fuss, Gene,' Abe Larkins protested. 'I ain't ready for a box yet.'

The Sharps spoke again. There was a hoarse cry and Matt raised his head in time to see a second Indian tumbling with part of his chest shot away.

'Damn!' Matt swore in frustration. The Apaches in the rocks returned the fire, but it was for show only. They would need to be a lot nearer to be effective.

'We could all end up like that,' Wilkes pointed out. 'I say we get out of here and get the army in, let them finish the Dukes off. You've proved your point. I'm convinced the Dukes killed Tom and Dan after what I've seen. What do you say, Abe?'

'I made a mistake, but I'm man enough to admit it.'

'We can ride out of here, let the Indians take care of the Dukes.' Sheriff Crow joined them. 'Without guns we ain't got a chance in hell and that's for sure.'

'The sheriff's right on both counts,' Wilkes agreed maliciously. 'If we get killed you hang for murder, Holder. You need us alive,' Wilkes pointed out what Matt already knew.

'Then I'll have to make sure you stay alive,' Matt replied.

'I see white men riding with Injuns. How can that be?' Across the rock strewn wasteland, amplified by the high, rock walls, floated Pappy Duke's nasal voice.

'They've come to see you and your boys die,' Matt shouted back.

There was a startled silence, then:

'Who's that?'

'Death,' Matt replied. 'I killed Billy, old man, and your turn's coming along with the rest of your lousy family.'

'Holder?' There was disbelief in the old man's voice. 'How'd you get outta that cave?'

'The hard way.'

'Guess I made a mistake in not killing you the first time.'

'You made a bigger mistake not killing me the second time.'

'Sure don't aim to make that mistake again.'

'You're pretty good with that Sharps. Did you use it on the two Larkins boys?'

'Seem to 'member that one sure could run. Almost got clean away. Took him on the ridge though.'

'What about the other one?'

'Figured he could outdraw Billy. What's your interest, boy? Seem to recall he didn't cotton on to you. Willing to pay $500 to see you dead. Ain't that something?'

Matt heard a groan from Abe Larkins. The old man sat there shaking his head. There were tears in his eyes when he looked up at Matt.

'So it was true. Sure Tom was a hothead, but to go that far . . . Pay to have you killed . . . .'

'It's over,' Matt said brusquely, not wanting the

man to torture himself. 'They paid the price, now it's time we collected.'

'You gonna sit there all day, boy?' Pappy taunted.

Abe Larkins looked across at Matt, eyes bright. 'Kill them, Holder. Don't let them get away,' he pleaded.

'I didn't come here to dance,' Matt replied grimly.

'Hey boy, why don't you show yourself?' Pappy called.

Matt's bearded lips compressed into a thin line. He looked around. His bay stood on the fringe of a group of Indian ponies. Matt whistled softly and the bay's ears pricked up. Matt called gently and the horse came across. When it was near enough, Matt took the trailing reins and led the beast deeper into the rocks until he could stand without being seen. From the saddlebags he took three pistols and tossed them towards Wilkes and the others.

'Your guns, gentlemen.' He climbed into the saddle. He had taken one other item from the saddlebags before mounting – the stick of dynamite – and thrust it into his coat pocket. He gathered up the reins and patted the bay's neck.

'What are you going to do?' Wilkes asked.

'Like the man said, I can't sit around here all day,' Matt replied and slapped the bay's rump. He felt the animal quiver and tense beneath him. Matt licked dry lips and tasted dust. His heart was hammering in his chest. Tightening the reins he dug both heels into the bay's flanks. The bay shot forward, kicking dust. Once clear of the rock jumble he hauled the bay to the right and sent it charging forward, a loud whooping cry exploding from his lips as an adrenalin surge charged his body up. Come hell or high water he had committed himself and was going to ride straight down Pappy Duke's throat.

THIRTEEN

On their rocky platform, protected by a natural wall, Rafe Duke saw the single rider break from the rocks and charge towards them.

'Rider coming, pa,' he shouted. 'It's that Holder fella!'

'Kin see him,' Pappy replied, as he sighted down the long barrel of the Sharps that rested on the wall. His boney finger was squeezing the trigger when the rider began to weave the horse from side to side and Pappy's shot went wide of the mark.

'You missed, pa,' Jack said, eyes wide.

'Hell, boy. I knowed I missed,' Pappy fumed, hurriedly reloading.

'The Injuns is on the move,' Rafe yelled. Running Fox had ordered his braves to remount as Matt had swept by and now, spread out in a ragged line, they thundered in Matt's wake yelling their war cries.

'He's gonna be in rifle range soon, so get to it, boys,' Pappy sang out. 'I'll see if'n I can't get me another Injun or two.'

When the Sharps bellowed gruffly again a brave to Red Cloud's right threw up his arms and fell from his

144

galloping horse. Matt had more than halved the distance between himself and the bluff when he reined the sweating bay to a stop behind a rock pile and slid from the saddle.

Matt heard the blood-freezing yells as he ran for the rocks and cast a quick look back as the Sharps spoke for a second time. He saw a brave to the far right leave his pony and smash into the rocks. He scrambled forward until he could see the bluff and levered off three quick shots before he was driven back by a fusillade of bullets that buzzed about his head like angry wasps. By now Running Fox and his braves had jumped from their ponies and had taken cover in the rocks that lay before the bluff. With lance in one hand, army-issue Spencer in the other, Red Cloud arrived behind Matt.

On the bluff Pappy Duke had forsaken the single shot Sharps for a Winchester. He had time to loose off two rounds before he and his boys were forced down into cover by a hail of bullets from below.

'What are we gonna do, pa?' Jack asked wildly.

'Do, boy? We ain't gonna mess our pants and that's for sure.' He squirmed his body into a sitting position, back to the wall, and dragged five sticks of dynamite from his coat pockets and tossed them down. 'We'll blow them redskins from here to hell.' He grinned as he fetched a match from his pocket and a stogie from another. Rafe and Jack smiled at each other as Pappy lit the stogie. After sucking the tip into red life Pappy picked up a stick of dynamite, touched the end of the cigar to the fuse and held the stick of dynamite at arm's length until half the fuse had burnt down. Rafe and Jack exchanged anxious glances as they watched their grinning father and waited for him to get rid of the dynamite before he blew them all to hell.

With a grunt and nod of satisfaction Pappy tossed the dynamite stick over his shoulder then scrambled onto his knees to risk a peep over the wall. He was rewarded with an eyeful of dust as a bullet glanced from the rock, inches from his head.

Matt saw the object spin against the blue sky, trailing a ragged tail of smoke, and, as it began to arc down, realized what it was. It was well to the left of his position. He saw it land amid rocks where two Apaches lay and a split second later the ground shook as the dynamite exploded. With a feeling of shock he saw two limp bodies fly out of a cloud of smoke and dust and whistling rock fragments. He ducked down dragging Red Cloud with him as seconds later sand and stone rained down on their position.

'You got two, pa,' Rafe shouted, laughing and whipping up his rifle to fire into the stunned Indians. Pappy Duke, rubbing the stinging dust from his red, tear-flowing eyes, managed to share Rafe's joy.

'We'll get a few more o' the red bastards, too,' he sang out.

Running Fox called his braves back, his small force of twenty now reduced to almost half. Matt slid back behind the rocks to join him.

'Their position's too good,' Matt declared stonily. 'They could hold an army off from up there.'

'We will wait,' Running Fox declared.

'Time we may not have,' Matt said. 'I gave the folk at Larkinsville a three-day deadline. If we are not back by then they'll send the Cavalry out. They may not wait that long.'

'What can we do, Matt Holder?' Red Cloud asked.

Matt eyed the young brave and the lance he carried.

'How good are you with that lance, Red Cloud?'

'Red Cloud has never been beaten in lance throwing.' Running Fox was quick to point this out, a touch of pride in his voice.

'That's good,' Matt said. 'Running Fox I need you and your braves to keep the Dukes occupied while Red Cloud and I circle to the west. If'n my idea works, then we'll be rid of the Dukes once and for all.'

'With a lance?' Running Fox looked puzzled.

'With a lance,' Matt agreed. He eyed Red Cloud. 'We stand a good chance of getting our fool heads blown off if we're spotted.'

'I go with you, Matt Holder,' Red Cloud replied stoutly.

'Swing your braves around to the east of the bluff, Running Fox. Keep up a steady covering fire, enough to make them keep their heads down. And don't get too close. He's probably got more dynamite up there. Here!' He thrust his Winchester into Running Fox's hands. 'You'll find three more cartons of shells in my saddlebags. Just keep the Dukes occupied.'

Running Fox gripped Matt's shoulder with a big

hand.

'May the Great Spirit watch over you, Matt Holder.'

'I second that,' Matt replied. 'Let's go, Red Cloud.' He looked back at Running Fox. 'One thing's for sure, you'll know if we succeed.'

'Where'd they all go?' Jack demanded, rubbing sweat from his eyes and face as he peered out over the deserted terrain. Minutes before it had been filled with screaming, yelling Apaches. Now it was as quiet and still as a grave. Jack didn't like it. In all the murderous forays and gunbattles he had been in before he had never felt so ill-at-ease. It didn't feel right, but he kept his mouth shut. Talk like that would have earned him a clip from Pappy.

''Paches are like that. Kin hide anywhere,' Pappy said with apparent unconcern.

'It's too damn quiet,' Jack moaned and a split second later a bullet chipped dust just inches from his head. He gave a wild yell and threw himself flat, much to the amusement of the other two.

'Thought you said it was quiet,' Rafe jeered. He peered over the top of the wall. 'I can see 'em. Moving to the east, circling to come in from a different direction.' Gunshots echoed from below and bullets buzzed and screamed, forcing them to take cover.

'Figure to keep us pinned down while a group come in from the east,' Pappy said. 'Well let's dust their tails a mite.' He picked up a stick of dynamite.

*   *   *

Matt and Red Cloud progressed through the rocks and gullies in a wide, flanking arc towards the western end of the bluff. They heard the dull, destructive explosion of dynamite amid the sporadic rifle fire. Matt hoped that Running Fox was keeping his braves back.

The bluff rose ahead. Its sides at this point were sheer and smooth rising some fifty feet up. In a small enclosed depression Matt sat on a sun-heated rock and pulled the stick of dynamite from his pocket.

'OK, Red Cloud, the rest is going to be up to you.' He took the Indian's lance, whipped the yellow bandanna from his neck and deftly tied the stick of dynamite to the shaft just below the point. 'We can gain height up ahead.' He pointed to a rearing jumble of boulders and rock slabs. 'Reckon we should be on the same level as the top of the bluff. Looks to me a good hundred feet, maybe a hundred-and-twenty. Can you pitch this thing right on top of the Dukes?'

Red Cloud took the lance and weighed it in his hand to assess the added weight, moving his hand forward a little to compensate for balance. He eyed the distance thoughtfully while Matt anxiously looked on and finally nodded.

'I can do it,' he said softly.

'On top of those rocks you'll be an easy target if they see you.' Matt pointed out and Red Cloud's lips twitched in a grim smile.

'We go,' he said and Matt smiled tensely.

The two clambered to the top of the rocks and cautiously lifted their heads the last few inches to peer over. From here they could see the three Dukes, hunkered down behind the wall at the far end of the bluff and Matt's heart jumped with elation. The three had their backs to them. Running Fox had done well to keep them occupied. Matt watched them for a few moments then nodded to Red Cloud. The young brave nodded back, face taut. Matt fished out a match, struck it on the rock and touched it to the fuse, put a hand on Red Cloud's shoulder to make him wait a few seconds. He took a quick look at the three, still with their backs to them and pulled his hand away.

'Go!' Matt said.

Red Cloud scrambled up and arose to his full height. He was making the most important throw of his life; the future of his tribe depended on it. If he overshot or fell short there would not be a second chance. The thought caused him to hesitate. Doubt flared in his eyes, but it was fleeting. He drew back his arm and launched the lance, dropping to one knee to watch its flight as it arced high against the blue sky and began to drop towards the bluff.

The first Pappy Duke knew of the lance was when it thudded into his back and he was slammed forward against the wall, his rifle spinning from his hands to the rocks below. He heard ribs crack as the point of the lance entered his left lung. It would have driven further through his body, but the dynamite stick prevented it.

'Damn it to hell,' he gasped, sitting back on his calves and tasting the metallic sting of hot blood in his throat that bubbled from his lips as he spoke. He could hear something hissing and the acrid smell of cordite bit into his nostrils. He shook dizziness from his head.

'You took a lance, pa,' Rafe breathed, backing away from the old man, terror in his eyes. Down below Running Fox had seen the lance fall, seen a figure jerk and the gun fall. Now he bade his braves to cease firing.

'Well help me, dammit,' Pappy cried, aware now that Jack had joined Rafe in retreat. 'I'm hurting bad.'

'There's dynamite tied to the lance, Pa,' Jack cried.

With great effort of will Pappy Duke lurched to his feet. By craning his head around he could glimpse the shaft of the lance angling from his back and smoke wisping up.

'You gotta help me, boys,' Pappy pleaded, terror in his eyes. He took a step forward holding his arms out to them. With a last, terrified look the two turned tail and bolted down the steep slope that led off the bluff preferring to take their chances with the Apaches rather than help Pappy. Pappy sank to his knees, blood rolling down his chin. 'Cowardly bastards!' he raved weakly and blew apart as the dynamite bound to the lance exploded.

Matt had not waited to see the outcome. When he saw Rafe and Jack turn tail he scrambled down from the rock pile.

Running and leaping over the uneven surface Matt reached the base of the bluff as Rafe and Jack emerged.

'Going somewhere, boys?' The Schofield-Smith and Wesson leapt into Matt's hand as he spoke. Rafe and Jack came to a hesitant halt. 'If you've a mind to make a play, go ahead; else drop the iron, boys,' Matt invited.

Rafe stared at Matt long and hard then with a snort tossed his rifle down and Jack followed.

'You turned Injun-lover now, Holder?' Rafe asked as Red Cloud joined Matt.

'Pistols, knives, dynamite. Shuck everything, boys. My finger's getting itchy.' As the two removed their gunbelts and Jack tossed his beloved knive onto the pile of hardware, Running Fox and his braves swarmed over the rocks venting cries of joy.

'He was the one that left me in the desert with hooks of iron in my flesh,' Red Cloud exclaimed pointing at Jack, anger hardening his voice. A group of young Apaches surrounded Jack.

'Get these damn savages off me, Holder,' Jack shouted.

'I got unfinished business with your brother, fat boy.' He looked at Rafe. 'Move.' He indicated towards a circular bed of sand that he had noticed earlier. Rock-free it measured maybe fifteen feet across. He halted Rafe at its edge. The Indians had followed, curious, Rafe was no less curious as Matt holstered his gun then silently removed his hat, coat and shirt.

'What's going on here, Holder?' Alarm tinged Rafe's voice.

In answer Matt immediately borrowed Red Cloud's broad-bladed hunting knife and tossed it into the centre of the sand circle.

'I intend to kill you with that knife, Duke,' Matt remarked casually and a mutter ran through the Indians. Rafe stared at Matt with his bulging, watery eyes, letting his glance dart to the knife then back again. He rasped a fist across his stubble-ringed lips. Then without warning he leapt onto the sand and dived for the knife, snatching it up and rising to a half-crouch, face triumphant.

'Mebbe I'll kill you,' he pointed out. 'Less'n you have help?'

'Just you and me, Duke,' Matt replied, removing his gunbelt and handing it to Red Cloud.

'What happens to me if'n I kill you?' Rafe wanted to know.

'You get the satisfaction of knowing you killed me before Running Fox here kills you.'

'Ain't much of a deal.'

'But the only one you've got.' Matt stepped onto the sand. 'More than you gave my son Ben, or the sisters at the Mission.' Matt stalked forward, feeling the cold rage build within him.

'Then we go to hell together!' Rafe roared and lunged at Matt, the blade glowing icily in the sunlight.

Rafe sliced upwards with a blow that had it struck would have split Matt from navel to chin, but the blade found only air to cut. Matt had swayed back out of danger and at the same time raised his right leg and with a jabbing kick drove a foot into Rafe's stomach. The man went backwards, doubled over, the air hissing from his lungs.

'You'll have to do better than that,' Matt goaded.

With a roar Rafe came forward, eyes glittering.

'I'm gonna enjoy sticking you, Holder,' he grunted. A crafty look came in his eyes. 'Like I enjoyed sticking those sisters.' He rubbed the front of his pants suggestively and grinned. 'Fresh, prime womanhood,' he gloated. He did not like Matt's calm approach. He needed to unsettle him. An angry man makes mistakes.

Matt felt white-hot anger burst through him as he circled the grinning man.

'Killing the boy was pure pleasure,' Rafe crooned happily.

Something snapped in Matt. He launched himself at the bigger man, blocking a knife-thrust only to have Rafe's left hand power into his stomach. He staggered back, winded, but not hurt, as Rafe flicked the knife into his left hand and threw himself at Matt. Matt blocked the knife-arm and deflected the fist that Rafe launched at him. He had nothing left to protect himself with as Rafe used his head, crashing his forehead against Matt's in a vicious butt. Matt saw stars and exploding lights as he flew backwards to slam down onto the hot sand, blood streaming from his forehead. He tried to shake the dizziness from his head as Rafe loomed, a blurry shape against the sky.

A boot slammed into Matt's side, cracking ribs and rolling him over. With a supreme effort he continued to roll until he could lurch unsteadily to his feet.

'You're dead meat, cowboy,' Rafe bragged. 'Dead

as your boy and them juicy sisters.' He grinned toothily, but this time Matt refused to be drawn. As the waves of dizziness faded, his face became hard, eyes soulless and dead, devoid of all emotion. He wiped blood from his forehead as Rafe came forward, tossing the knife back and forth from one hand to the other. The big man was sure he had Matt weakened enough to inflict more injury before he finally killed him. Rafe reflected that if he was going to die anyway he'd rest a lot easier knowing he'd taken Holder with him. His dreams were rudely shattered. In a series of moves that gave Rafe the impression he was fighting ten men and not one, Matt went into action using hands and feet.

Matt went through Rafe's guard to deliver punishing straight-fingered blows to Rafe's throat and edge-of-hand blows that drove the man back. In graceful, controlled leaps Matt delivered devastating kicks to Rafe's body. The half-circle of Apaches, no mean close-combat fighters themselves, watched in silent awe as Matt slowly demolished his opponent with his strange fighting manner.

Rafe was beaten to his knees without landing a single blow on Matt. Blood ran from his nose and lips and his body felt as though it had been run over by a wagon. Unable to comprehend what was happening to him he stared with blurred vision at his tormentor, reduced to a dark shadow. Matt scooped up the knife Rafe had lost earlier.

'He's got the knife, Rafe. Get up!' Jack raved. Rafe heard the warning and stiffened, pawing at his eyes to clear them.

A blurred shadow moved before Rafe. He shook his head and the shape took on features and cold, grey eyes stared down from a bearded face. Eyes that appeared cold and lifeless — merciless.

'No more,' Rafe croaked. 'No more.' Sunlight reflected from the knife in Matt's hand into his eyes.

'Did the sisters beg, Duke? Did they plead as you raped and murdered them?' Matt's voice battered his ears and he let his head droop. 'Ben never even got a chance to plead for his life.' Matt took a handful of hair and tilted the man's face up. An eight-year-old boy that never had the chance to become a man.' Matt's voice shook. 'You put a bullet in his head and laughed while you did it.'

Rafe stared with hate at Matt then, with a sudden surge of energy, he hauled himself to his feet knocking Matt's grip on his hair aside and wrapping his arms about Matt's body, forgetting the knife Matt held. He remembered it at the last moment, but by then it was too late. He grunted and his eyes opened wide as the blade slid between his ribs. Matt held on to the knife as Rafe sank, coughing blood, to his knees. He gave Matt a final, hate-filled stare, then fell forward and lay still.

It was over at last; the quest for revenge fulfilled. But was it a hollow victory, Matt wondered, as the Apaches crowed around howling their approval? So many innocent people had died.

FOURTEEN

Matt reined the bay to a halt two miles south of Larkinsville. Here the trail continued south or cut east towards the Pecos river.

Two weeks had passed since the battle in the hidden valley, since Matt had ridden from the valley with Abe Larkins, Judge Wilkes and Sheriff Crow. The four had ridden unaccompanied, turning deaf ears to the high pitched, tortured screams that chased across the valley in their wake as the Apaches remained behind with Jack Duke.

They had run into a cavalry patrol at the Mission, but Abe Larkins had managed to sort out the little 'misunderstanding' reported by the good people of Larkinsville. On returning to Larkinsville all charges had been dropped against Matt. As an added extra Wilkes and Sheriff Crow had seen to it that Matt received the full reward money for the Dukes.

In that two weeks Matt had buried Seth Coggins and Abe Larkins had taken Clara under his wing.

'Stay in Larkinsville, Matt,' Abe Larkins offered, but Matt had declined the offer. There were too many memories attached to the town. With a rueful smile Matt turned the bay's head east.

West of the Pecos had proved a difficult ride for Matt; maybe east of the Pecos would smile more kindly on him.